THE K TEAM

DAVID ROSENFELT

MINOTAUR
BOOKS
NEW YORK

This is a work of fiction. All of the characters, organizations, and events portrayed in this novel are either products of the author's imagination or are used fictitiously.

Published in the United States by Minotaur Books, an imprint of St. Martin's Publishing Group

 Printed in the United States of America. For information, address St. Martin's Publishing Group, 120 Broadway, New York, NY 10271.

www.minotaurbooks.com

Designed by Omar Chapa

The Library of Congress has cataloged the hardcover edition as follows:

Names: Rosenfelt, David, author.
Title: The K team / David Rosenfelt.
Description: First edition. | New York : Minotaur Books, 2020.
Identifiers: LCCN 2019047328 | ISBN 9781250257192 (hardcover) |
ISBN 9781250257185 (ebook)
Subjects: GSAFD: Mystery fiction.
Classification: LCC PS3618.O838 K15 2020 | DDC 813/.6—dc23
LC record available at https://lccn.loc.gov/2019047328

ISBN 978-1-250-77965-6 (trade paperback)

First Minotaur Books Trade Paperback Edition: 2021

10 9 8 7 6 5 4 3 2 1

Praise for David Rosenfelt

"One of the most unforgettable authors in the genre."

—Associated Press

"[Rosenfelt] has been more than one kind of writer in his life, and never fails to deliver full value." —*Sullivan County Democrat*

"Rosenfelt, like Dick Francis, keeps coming up with inventive ways to ensnare his hero in cases involving animals." —*Kirkus Reviews*

"David Rosenfelt never disappoints!" —*Fresh Fiction*

Praise for *The K Team*

"Corey serves as an investigator and narrator every bit as ebullient as Andy and a lot more diligent. . . . If you liked Rosenfelt's rollicking previous series, you'll like this one too." —*Kirkus Reviews*

"David Rosenfelt is a master of the mystery/suspense genre and with *The K Team* he has launched a new and inherently entertaining series." —*Midwest Book Review*

"I'm happy as a clam to keep reading the Andy Carpenter books, and now have the K Team books to add to my reading enjoyment. Highly recommended." —*Deadly Pleasures*

"David Rosenfelt has written an excellent first entry to his second series. . . . It's told in a fresh voice by a sympathetic protagonist who will draw you into the book and keep you engrossed until the end." —*Marilyn's Mystery Reads*

"[An] engaging series launch." —*Stop, You're Killing Me!*

ALSO BY DAVID ROSENFELT

ANDY CARPENTER NOVELS

Silent Bite

Muzzled

Dachshund Through the Snow

Bark of Night

Deck the Hounds

Rescued

Collared

The Twelve Dogs of Christmas

Outfoxed

Who Let the Dog Out?

Hounded

Unleashed

Leader of the Pack

One Dog Night

Dog Tags

New Tricks

Play Dead

Dead Center

Sudden Death

Bury the Lead

First Degree

Open and Shut

THRILLERS

Black and Blue

Fade to Black

Blackout

Without Warning

Airtight

Heart of a Killer

On Borrowed Time

Down to the Wire

Don't Tell a Soul

NONFICTION

Lessons from Tara: Life Advice from the World's Most Brilliant Dog

Dogtripping: 25 Rescues, 11 Volunteers, and 3 RVs on Our Canine Cross-Country Adventure

THE K TEAM

IT WAS THE TYPE OF SITUATION JOHN LOWRY KNEW HE SHOULD AVOID.

He was at Rafferty's Bar in Passaic; one of eight patrons left, which could be considered a healthy number since it was two thirty in the morning. Lowry remembered a football coach named Herm Edwards saying, "Nothing good ever happened after two A.M.," but in truth Lowry was aware of that long before Edwards said it.

Plenty of bad things had happened to Lowry at that time of the morning over the years, and almost every one of them was Lowry's fault. He had a temper, maybe the shortest fuse of anyone he had ever known, and alcohol made it even shorter. Rafferty's Bar, not surprisingly, sold alcohol.

So though Lowry had long ago resolved to avoid situations like this, he had frequently ignored that resolution. But the reality was that showing discipline, while always a weak point for Lowry, had suddenly become far more important than ever before.

It was going to take a year, maybe longer, but he was going to be rich. Not just rich, incredibly rich. Never work again, never worry again . . . that kind of rich. In fact, his visit to the bar that night was ironically a celebration of the events of that day.

He had proven himself to the people he needed to impress, the people who would become his partners. They would supply the money, the organization, and the expertise. But he was absolutely essential to the process, as he had demonstrated today.

The other irony is that Lowry was acting honorably. He saw a couple arguing in a booth. The woman looked scared of the guy, and as it turned out, she had a right to be.

He was a big man, at least as big as Lowry, which meant he was very big. Lowry was six-four, two forty, and although the guy was sitting down, he looked to be just as tall and maybe even heavier. The difference between the guy and Lowry was that the guy had some layers of fat, and Lowry did not.

Lowry was in outstanding shape because he worked at it. He started his adult life as a boxer, but after winning only twelve of twenty fights, he realized that his possessing knockout power in both hands was not going to be enough. He exited the fight game and never looked back, but he took with him a strong workout ethic.

Lowry liked working out, liked how it made him feel. The guy in the booth clearly did not share that view. He obviously liked eating; liked how it made him feel.

As Lowry watched from his vantage point at the other side of the room, the guy suddenly reached across the table and smacked the woman in the face. Not with anywhere close to full force, but enough to draw some blood at the side of her mouth, and more than enough to make her cry.

And way more than enough to piss Lowry off.

So he went over to the table and said to the guy in a controlled voice, not at all slurred from alcohol, "I'll tell you what you're going to do, asshole. You're going to stand up and get out of here. She stays."

The guy stood up, but was not inclined to obey. Instead, he was inclined to say, "Why don't you try and make me leave?"

Lowry's voice remained calm. "I'll give you one more opportunity to make the right decision. You can walk out or be carried out. It's your choice, but hurry up. I don't want to spend more time with you than I have to."

The woman, no longer sobbing, said, "Randy—"

It was impossible to know what she was going to say because Randy said, "Shut up, Carla." He then turned back to Lowry, his fists already clenched, and said, "Beat it, dipshit."

Lowry's short fuse was thereby lit, and the short right cross followed seconds later. It landed a little too perfectly. In the ring, with gloves on, it would have accomplished its mission and hurt the opponent, probably even knocking him down or out.

In this case, in Rafferty's Bar at two thirty in the morning and with no gloves on, it drove Randy's chin and nose up into his head, puncturing his brain and sending him back into his seat in the booth.

Dead.

The police arrived within minutes, and Lowry was taken into custody. He knew all too well he was going down for this; people must have seen him throw the first and only punch. Carla certainly had seen it all. Lowry could be going away for a long time.

In the blink of an eye, it had gone from being the best day of John Lowry's life to the worst.

WE CALL OURSELVES THE K TEAM.

The name wasn't my idea; I didn't even think we needed a name. One of my partners, Laurie Collins, thought we should have one, and she came up with K Team. I'm fine with it, but I would also have been fine without it. My name is Corey Douglas and people know me as an easygoing guy, except when I'm not.

Actually, I'm not usually a team kind of guy, and the last team I was on that had a name was back in Little League, right here in Paterson, New Jersey. We were called the 10th Avenue Citizens, which in retrospect seems pretty bizarre, since I don't recall any of us living on Tenth Avenue.

The other members of the K team are Marcus Clark and Simon Garfunkel. Marcus has become something of a legend here in the Paterson, New Jersey, area. I'm told he's a good investigator, but that's not what he's known for. He's going to be our muscle, our enforcer, for lack of better words, because he is known for being the toughest, scariest guy on the planet, and he combines that with an apparent lack of both conscience and fear.

It's probably good that Marcus is on our side.

Simon Garfunkel is a German shepherd. He and I worked together as members of the Paterson Police Department until last month. I retired, and after much resistance, the powers that be caved and let Simon retire with me. We're as close as two buddies can be, and Simon might be the best cop I ever worked with.

Simon pretty much defines friendship and teamwork, at least as I see it. We give each other space, but we're there for each other when the chips are down. In the business we were in, the cop business, the chips were down fairly often. The next time Simon lets me down, or I let him down, will be the first.

The K Team has only been in existence for two weeks, so we haven't had any actual cases or assignments to work on yet. I haven't minded because after twenty-five years on the force I could use a break. Having said that, I'm sure my desire to be active will kick in any minute, as will my desire to earn money.

Both desires may be satisfied pretty soon. Laurie and I are at my old hunting grounds, the downtown headquarters of the Paterson Police Department, for a meeting with Pete Stanton, the captain in charge of the Homicide Division. Pete had called Laurie and asked to meet with us on an important matter, without going into any more detail about it. Laurie used to be with Paterson PD also, as a lieutenant, so we both know our way around here.

The strange part about it is that he said that while it wasn't necessary for Marcus to come along, he insisted that Andy Carpenter be here. In addition to being Laurie's husband, Andy is a smart, annoying, talented, sarcastic, successful, and irritating criminal defense attorney, probably the most famous that Paterson has to offer. Of course, that's a low bar; Paterson has never been known as a breeding ground for big-time lawyers.

Andy is not technically a part of our team, though we will be doing his investigative work when he takes on a case. He is not at all eager to take on clients, which is why I left "hardworking" out of my description of him.

My experiences with Andy have been mixed, to say the least. A few years ago he chewed me up in a cross-examination during a murder trial, and I strongly considered shooting him in revenge. There isn't a cop or judge in New Jersey that would have blamed me; Andy is not exactly worshiped by the law enforcement community.

I'm glad I let him live, because he recently sued the police department on Simon's behalf, earning him the first early retirement in Paterson K-9 cop history. It was a brilliant piece of lawyering, and it's accurate to say that Andy is the reason Simon is a member of our team and isn't still working nine-to-five as a cop.

I'm grateful to Andy for doing that, even though I know he was doing it for Simon, and not for me. Andy is a dog lover; in addition to he and Laurie having two of their own, he co-runs a dog rescue organization as a hobby.

So in addition to not knowing why Pete called this meeting, I have no idea why he wanted Andy to be a part of it. I know they are friends and share a regular table at Charlie's Sports Bar, but I'm pretty sure we're not here on a social call.

Andy is supposed to meet Laurie and me here, but he hasn't arrived yet, and we get called in to meet with Pete. I'm surprised when we get back there and Pete is alone; I would have thought he'd have at least one other officer in the meeting, just to keep a record of what is said. There must be something confidential about this.

"Hey, guys. Thanks for coming." Pete gives Laurie a quick kiss on the cheek. Fortunately he limits his greeting of me to a handshake. Then, "Where's Andy?"

"Right here." Andy comes into the office as if on cue. He looks around the messy office. "I love what you've done with the place." Then, "What am I doing here?"

"It wasn't my idea, believe me," Pete says.

"Why don't you tell us why we're all here?" I say, trying to move this along.

Pete nods. "Okay, but before I do, I should tell you that the only other person in the department who knows about this meeting is the chief. And I'm relying on your honor that if you aren't interested in what I am about to say, then you will keep all of this in confidence."

Laurie and I look at each other, and we both give reluctant nods.

"Okay," Laurie says. "Dependent, of course, on what it is you have to say."

"I'm not going to confess to a felony, if that's what you mean," Pete says. "There is someone who wants to meet with you. A potential client."

"I'm retired," Andy says.

Pete nods. "I can only hope the justice system will survive without you. But either way, you're not a participant in this in any meaningful way. So even though it goes against your history and everything you stand for, I suggest you shut up and listen."

"Who's the client?" Laurie asks.

"Judge Henry Henderson."

I'm sure we're all surprised, but it's Andy who speaks first. "Hatchet?"

Pete nods. "The very one."

I know Judge Henderson in that I've testified in cases over which he presided. He's always struck me as tough but fair. That toughness usually comes out when he is dealing with lawyers;

he's never seemed fond of them. "Why is he called Hatchet?" I ask.

Andy fields the question. "Because it is said that he chops the testicles off lawyers. I can't say whether that's true, but when he walks, you can hear stuff rattling in his pockets. They ain't Tic Tacs, that's for sure."

"Do you want to hear the rest?" Pete asks. It's a general question, aimed at Laurie and me.

"I'm not defending him, I can tell you that," Andy says.

"That's the first accurate thing you've said since I've known you," Pete says. "As I previously mentioned, you are not a key player here; try to manage your ego and understand that."

Then Pete turns to Laurie and me. "The Judge wants to meet with you. Andy is invited for that first meeting only. Hatchet, I mean, Judge Henderson, will explain everything. I would tell you more if I knew more, which I don't. My job was to set up the meeting."

"When?" Laurie asks.

"Now. The Judge is waiting for you at his home."

IT TAKES LESS THAN TWENTY MINUTES TO DRIVE TO JUDGE HENDERSON'S house in Fair Lawn.

It's in a nice but unexceptional suburban neighborhood, the kind of place where people take pride in their lawns being neatly mowed, and where weeds are viewed as a mortal enemy.

We've come here in two cars because that's how many we had at Pete's office. Laurie drove with me rather than Andy, which I think is a sign of her being a team player, rather than an unhappy wife. Andy didn't seem to mind; I think he was too busy minding that he was involved in this in the first place.

As we walk up onto the porch, the Judge opens the door to let us enter. He doesn't say a word, although both Laurie and I give half-hearted hellos. The only expression I can see on his face is a slight sneer at Andy. I'm assuming there's a history there, but Andy is on the invited list, so maybe there is also some respect.

"Anything to drink?" is the first thing Hatchet says.

Laurie and I decline, and Andy says, "I'll have a nonfat, venti, decaf cappuccino with extra foam. And maybe a raspberry scone, but warm it up first."

That gets no reaction from anyone except an eye roll from Laurie. The Judge tells us to follow him into the den and then to sit down. So we follow and sit; I think people have a tendency to do what Judge Henderson says.

"First some ground rules," the Judge says, speaking with such authority that I expect him to pound a gavel. "I am considering hiring the group that I understand calls themselves the K Team, though the fact that you've chosen a childish name like that causes me to preemptively question my decision. Nevertheless, both the chief and Captain Stanton have recommended you. The fact that you will be employed in this effort by Mr. Carpenter makes it particularly attractive."

"Aw, shucks. All this time I never realized how much you were impressed by me," Andy says.

"Don't flatter yourself. Your involvement ends with this meeting. But you are an attorney, so if I hire you, and then you hire them as investigators, they are subject to the same ironclad attorney-client confidentiality. Because in this matter I insist on strict confidentiality."

"That hurts," Andy says.

"As a result of this, of course, the resulting conflict will mean that I will never again be able to preside over a case in which you are the defense attorney."

Andy nods. "That eases the pain somewhat."

The Judge hands Andy a dollar. "So you are now officially my attorney, at least for the moment. Does everybody understand the implications of this?"

Laurie and I both nod. "This question requires a verbal response," the Judge says, so Laurie and I both give him one. Andy doesn't, but Henderson doesn't push it. Instead he nods and says, "Good. I received this three days ago."

He removes an envelope from his desk drawer and takes a piece of paper out, handing it to us. It's a message printed in clear block letters: "Soon you will be called upon to do us a service, and you will deliver. You have already been well paid, and we have other proof as well. Don't make us show it to you."

The questions are obvious, and Laurie asks them: "Do you know who this is from?"

"No."

"Do you know what they mean by a 'service'?"

"No."

"Do you know what they mean when they say you have been 'well paid'?"

I am expecting another quick no, but that's not what we get. Instead Hatchet reaches into the same envelope and pulls out another piece of paper. It is a bank statement from an account in the Cayman Islands, in the name of Henry Henderson. "This came with it."

I look carefully at the statement, which is from last month. It shows a wire-transfer deposit of $20,000, which is the only entry of any kind for the month. The balance at the bottom shows that this deposit brings the total in the account to in excess of $390,000.

"I was sent the other statements as well," the Judge says. "It shows that someone has been depositing the same amount in this account for at least eighteen months. Interest has accrued."

My turn to do the questioning. "Did you open the account?"

"Of course not."

"When did you find out about it?"

"Three days ago."

"And no idea who sent this to you?"

"Asked and answered," he says, showing some frustration.

"Have you ever been to the Caymans or had contact with any entity or person there?"

"No."

"Do you know how they could have opened this account without your knowledge?"

"That would be one of the things for you to find out, if you decide to accept the assignment."

I certainly am in favor of taking the job. First of all, it's intriguing, and second of all, it's a job. I look at Laurie, and her slight nod indicates her agreement. We should probably talk about it with Marcus as well, but even in the unlikely event that he is opposed, he's already outvoted. Andy doesn't have a vote and doesn't show any desire to weigh in.

"We're in," I say, then run through our fees.

The Judge says, "Fine; I will give you a retainer. I want to be kept up-to-date on all developments. But I want no personal involvement whatsoever. I need to stay out of any physical presence in this."

"We'll do our best to keep you in the loop," Laurie says, "but you can't micromanage this. We are professionals."

Henderson nods. "I understand. I am a professional as well, with a professional reputation that must be considered and protected. That is what this is about."

"It is also about extortion and blackmail," I say.

"Thank you for sharing that," Henderson says, so dryly that the words come out parched. "Now please get to work."

KEVIN VICKERS WATCHED LAURIE, ANDY, AND COREY LEAVE HENDERSON'S house.

He did so from the comfort of his car, more than half a block away. Vickers wore what would have seemed to a passerby to be ordinary glasses, but they were actually telescopic lenses. Vickers could only imagine how expensive they were, but he knew that the people he was working for could easily afford them.

He did not know the identity of the three visitors, but that would be easy enough to find out. They did not look like cops—the clothing and the cars were giveaways on that front.

Vickers took pictures of them going in and coming out. He would report in, send the photos to his employer, who would easily have the resources and wherewithal to find out who they were. They pretty much had the resources to do anything.

So far this had been the easiest and most lucrative job Vickers had ever had. He imagined there would be tougher, more dangerous days ahead, but that was not a concern.

Vickers could handle whatever came his way.

For now Vickers did as he was supposed to do and called his boss to alert him to what was happening. He called him on his office phone, which he considered strange, since it could easily be traced. He only knew the boss as Ellis and didn't even know if that was his first or last name, or if that was his real name. Vickers doubted that it was.

Ellis never answered the phone; a machine always picked up. But he always called back within one minute. Vickers did not understand why that was, but it didn't matter to him.

This time Ellis listened with interest to what Vickers had to say, told him to stay on the Judge, and hung up. The information Vickers had provided was interesting. The Judge going to someone other than the police for help meant that he was not precluding anything. Had he brought the police in, then it would have demonstrated that he had decided not to give in to the demands. Keeping it private left open the possibility that he might ultimately cooperate, though that was still highly unlikely.

Either way, it wouldn't matter.

I LIVE ON EAST THIRTY-THIRD STREET IN PATERSON, OFF NINETEENTH Avenue.

The east side of Paterson has a simple economic structure. The neighborhoods get nicer, and the people living in them more economically advantaged, as the street numbers get higher. Forty-second street is the highest; if you live beyond that, you're on a houseboat in the Passaic River. Nobody wants to live in the Passaic River, not even fish.

Laurie and Andy live on Forty-second Street; they are known to be wealthy, both from a large inheritance that Andy received from his father and from some lucrative cases he has handled. As a cop who is the son of a cop who was the son of a cop, I had neither of those. Money has never been particularly important to me, which comes in handy, since I've never had much of it.

In recognition of all this, Laurie took the lead in setting up our K Team financial partnership. Marcus will get 40 percent of all revenue, I will get 50, and she will take 10. Basically she said that she feels it's important that she be paid for her work; she just doesn't care how much.

It was obviously generous and considerate of her to do that, but not surprising considering her reputation. She and I knew each other during the years we were both on the force, but it was more of a "nodding good morning" relationship. I don't recall us ever working a case together. But I have a bunch of friends who know her well and have nothing but great things to say about her.

I will get more than Marcus because I am responsible for the care of Simon Garfunkel, our fourth team member. Marcus had no problem with the arrangement, and it was all done on a series of handshakes.

I like my teammates.

A lot.

I've headed home after the meeting with Judge Henderson, since Simon has to be walked. Laurie is dropping Andy off at their house and then heading here, and Marcus is on his way as well. We need to begin to plot out a strategy for investigating this case.

Simon and I do a fairly quick walk; we go to School Number 20, the local grammar school I attended decades ago. Simon likes to walk around the ball field behind the school, but I don't give him much time to do so today, so that we can get back to meet Laurie and Marcus.

Simon's a happy guy, always smiling and seeming to enjoy life. He particularly likes other dogs and always brightens when he runs into one on our walks. The only time he did not appear happy was when he was working as a police dog. Then he'd have on his game face, and then he was one badass dog.

You would not want to mess with Simon when he's working.

When we get back, Marcus is waiting on the porch and Laurie is just pulling up. "Sorry to keep you waiting," I say to Marcus.

His response is something like "Ynnhh." In the short time I've known him, I've learned that Marcus is a man of few words, none of them remotely understandable. Laurie seems able to communicate with him, which makes one of us.

Simon has already grown to like Marcus and runs to him to receive his expected petting. Marcus seems happy to oblige. We head inside; I give all three of them water and throw in a biscuit for Simon, and then we're ready.

Laurie updates Marcus on the conversation with Judge Henderson. Marcus listens without saying a word, without showing any reaction. I assume he's heard and understood everything, but I can't be sure. Laurie and Andy both have said that people underestimate Marcus's intelligence, that he's really smart. I can't be sure of that either; I haven't yet seen evidence either way.

Once she is finished, Laurie asks of no one in particular, "So what do we know?"

"We know that Henderson is going to be blackmailed into performing a service, and I think we can assume that it will be in his judicial capacity," I say. "And we know that there has been an elaborate and expensive plot to create a scenario in order to frame him for acts that they will allege he has already committed."

Laurie nods. "Right. And we know that this plot has been in existence for at least eighteen months, so we are dealing with people who are patient and who have very substantial resources. What don't we know?"

"That's a longer list," I say. "We don't know who is doing it, why they are doing it, what are the additional things they have that they say they can use to frame him with, what is the service they will be asking him to perform, and when will they be asking him."

Laurie says, "As far as the when question goes, I think we can assume it will be soon. There would otherwise be no other reason to alert and prepare him now. They've gone at least eighteen months without saying anything; they wouldn't break their silence now unless it was either imminent or close to it."

"It has to be related to an upcoming case for the Judge."

Laurie frowns. "That's a little complicated; I talked to Andy about it on the way home. He called the court clerk, and the next case on the Judge's calendar is a domestic violence assault. It's apparently going to last less than a week, and he has nothing listed after that."

"Who decides what cases he gets?"

"According to Andy, he does. He's the chief judge; he doles them out both for himself and all the judges under him. So there's a possibility that whatever the blackmailers are concerned about won't be his case at all. The blackmailer may simply want to dictate which judge gets a particular case; it might be that one of the other judges is already in his pocket."

"I would doubt that. But for now, all we can do is accumulate as much information as we can."

She nods. "Which brings us to Sam Willis. He can get the information from the Caymans; we can't. Or at least it would take so long it wouldn't be worth getting."

She's talking about trying to find out the circumstances behind the setting up of the bank account. "The Judge could make the request," I say. "It's technically his account, whether he was involved with setting it up or not."

"He made it clear he will not take any proactive steps, and in this case I don't blame him. It's best he not have any actual involvement with this account. Sam is our best—and probably only—avenue to pursue."

We have discussed the Sam Willis situation in general terms, and it is the first internal disagreement we have had, though there will no doubt be others. Sam is an accountant and handles the books for Andy's firm. But when Sam goes into a phone booth, should they exist anymore, he changes into Super-Hacker.

According to Laurie, he can get into virtually any computer anywhere and has been invaluable to Andy on many cases. The problem is that it is mostly illegal to get into any computer anywhere. That apparently doesn't bother Andy, and while Laurie is uncomfortable with it, my disdain for the process is much more intense.

As a cop I was known as something of a hard-ass, which means I was a stickler who did things by the book. The few exceptions over the years resulted from my considerable temper overcoming my rationality, at least in the moment.

"You know how I feel about this," I say.

She nods. "Yes, I know, and for the most part I agree. But here's the other way to look at it. First of all, we should consider Sam's potential involvement on a case-by-case basis, and only if there are no viable alternatives. Second, we should and will only use any information we get in the pursuit of justice."

"We are not the people that get to decide what is justice and what isn't."

"But in this instance we can, and we are well equipped to do it. Lastly, we will only acquire information that we can also acquire legally as part of a judicial proceeding and would at a later date if we need to. This just speeds up the process, which is necessary."

"That's a rationalization."

She nods. "It is. But it also makes sense."

I'm not happy about this, but I am going to lose the argument. "Okay, but we discuss these things case by case, and you deal with Sam."

Laurie nods. "Agreed. Marcus?"

"Ynnh."

"Good," she says. "Let's get to work."

BEING AN EX-COP HAS ITS ADVANTAGES.

Not as many as being an ex-CEO, or an ex–NFL quarterback, but there are a few perks, especially for cops turned private investigators.

I'm taking advantage of one of them now. It's five o'clock, and it would normally be the end of the workday for Sergeant Xavier Jennings of the Paterson PD. After thirty-five years, Xavier has reached legendary status in forensics, and as he nears retirement, he's going to be tough to replace.

I've brought with me the documents that Judge Henderson received from his potential blackmailer. The Judge handled them fairly carelessly, and I held them myself, since when he handed them to me, I had no idea they could be evidence.

So I doubt we'll get prints or anything else of value off of them. If the perpetrator took Blackmail 101 or read *Extortion for*

Dummies, then there would not have been any usable forensics anyway. But it's worth a shot.

I don't tell Xavier the story behind any of the documents, and I doubt that he's even interested enough to read them. He's only concerned with any prints or DNA that could be on them. I do tell him that everything is confidential, which is unnecessary but makes me feel better.

We talk a bit about retirement. Xavier has some trepidation about it, as I did. We've both done the job for so long that it's a bit scary to be staring into what seems like a large, empty abyss. Everybody reacts differently, and I hope Xavier handles it well. I have, but then again, I'm much younger than him and I've just switched jobs. Xavier is quitting cold turkey.

I don't have time to sit and chat with Xavier for long, so I leave the stuff with him. He promises he'll have answers for me tomorrow. For now I've got to get home, walk Simon, and get dressed to go out.

I've got a date.

I've spent my life simultaneously having excellent and minimal success with women. I'm considered good-looking by mostly everyone except my bathroom mirror. Women respond to me; I think they mistakenly view my quiet insecurity as evidence that I am the strong, silent type.

So when I'm so inclined, I have little trouble meeting women and getting them to go out with me. That then triggers the other problem, which is that once they go out with me, the clock starts ticking until the time I want them to stop going out with me.

I guess it's a classic fear of commitment, though I honestly don't know where it comes from. My parents had a remarkably happy thirty-seven-year marriage, and theirs was a terrific home to grow up in. Maybe the problem is that as a cop I have been witness to my share of domestic troubles, often culminating in violence.

Like I say, I have no idea. I'm sure that many people would suggest I talk to a therapist about it. A number of women that I've dated have made that exact suggestion, usually in a loud, exasperated, angry voice. And there is certainly a chance that I will sit in a stranger's office, talk about my most personal feelings, and pay for the privilege. There is also a chance that I will sing opera at the Met and tunnel my way to China with a spoon.

But while I can't say exactly why, I do know that when I start to date a woman, if it does not go well, then I don't want to keep seeing her. If it goes well, then I worry about the long-term implications, so I don't want to keep seeing her. So bad is bad and good is bad. It doesn't leave me with much to root for.

Tonight I am seeing Dani Kendall. It's our ninth or tenth date, I'm not sure which, but either one breaks my all-time record. She's pretty perfect . . . smart, funny, beautiful, independent, nondemanding. I knew most of that within the first ten minutes of my meeting her, which means I knew this was a disaster from the start.

So I've semiconsciously been searching for that transgression that will cause me to bring this thing to a screeching halt. Maybe she'll make some comment that I can interpret as revealing a previously hidden prejudice? Maybe she'll try to change me or become overly critical? Maybe she'll unveil an annoying habit, like cracking her knuckles? Maybe I'll find evidence implicating her in serial murders? Maybe anything?

So far no luck, which is why this doomed relationship is still steaming full speed ahead. Tonight we're meeting at Dantoni's, a neighborhood Italian place in Ridgefield Park. We've been here four times, so it's becoming "our place." The problem is that I don't want to have a "place" with anyone. So while I love the pasta, I am determined to make this our farewell appearance here.

Dani is sitting at the bar waiting for me when I arrive. She's never late, still another "good-therefore-bad" trait of hers. The conversation is easy and enjoyable; we even share a love of both the Mets and the Giants. We don't talk much about each other's job; she is an event planner for a PR firm.

As always, everything is completely comfortable. I look forward to seeing her, and when I do, I am never disappointed.

Like I said, this is a total train wreck.

While we're having coffee, I have my hand resting on the table. Dani puts her hand on mine and says, "So where are we going, Corey?"

I tense up like someone stuck an electric prod up my ass. I choke out the words "You know I don't like to talk about the future, Dani. Or predict it. Or think about it. What is going to happen is going to happen."

She smiles. "I was talking about next Friday."

"Friday?"

She nods. "Yes. You told me that we are going someplace, but it's a surprise. Is it too scary to look ahead to Friday?"

"Oh," I say, because I can't think of anything else. Then, "Friday's good. I can deal with Friday."

"So what are we doing?"

"We're going to an Eagles concert at Madison Square Garden." The Eagles are Dani's favorite band.

"We are?"

I nod. "Floor seats."

"I knew I was dating you for a reason."

"I thought it was my boyish charm."

She shakes her head. "Not even close."

We end the night at my house. We used to alternate between mine and Dani's, but I always felt guilty leaving Simon alone. She likes Simon, which is a good thing for the future, which means it's a somewhat bad thing.

I think.

I'm a bit confused.

XAVIER JENNINGS CALLS AT EIGHT IN THE MORNING.

He doesn't interrupt anything between Dani and me because she left at midnight last night. We haven't quite gotten to the staying-over stage. I'm not sure whose idea that was or is; we just both seem okay with it.

I drove her home, like I always do. I may be opposed to commitment, but I'm pro-chivalry.

Xavier sounds excited, or at least intrigued. "We got some prints. Two sets. Waiting on DNA."

"Could you ID the prints?"

"Absolutely. One set is yours."

"Wonderful. I suspected myself all along. Who is the other one?"

"None other than Judge Henry Henderson."

The Judge's name had been on the Caymans bank statement,

but we had redacted it, so Xavier would have no reason to expect the Judge's fingerprints to be on it.

I swear Xavier to secrecy and ask him to let me know if the DNA results show anything else, though I'm fairly confident they won't. I thank him for his efforts and hang up.

The blackmailer was smart enough not to leave any prints; the Judge and I weren't. Bad guys one—good guys zero.

I call Laurie to tell her the forensic results. "No surprise there," she says. "I put Sam on the account in the Caymans. There's more chance we'll get something out of that, because the people that set it up would be confident they could keep it secret."

"We may be heading for a situation where all we can do is wait for someone to make a move. That's not my favorite position to be in."

"I agree. But in the meantime we can try and figure out who that someone is."

"Have we gotten the court records?" I ask.

"Marcus is on it," she says. "We should have it in a day or two."

"I would think Andy could help with it."

"The Judge doesn't want Andy involved and I think we should honor that. Although he did tell the court clerk that Marcus would be making a request, and that he'd appreciate them hurrying it."

We will be looking at all of Judge Henderson's cases for the last three years, with special emphasis on eighteen months ago, when the payments started. Our hope is to find something that the bad guys can claim Henderson handled unethically, maybe intentionally so.

It's even possible that the entire case is about revenge for something the Judge did to some previous defendant before him.

If the blackmail is for an alleged indiscretion in the Judge's past, it's possible that something will jump out at us that could appear suspicious.

"What about future cases?" I ask.

"According to Andy, there will be some that would automatically go to whatever judge might have been involved in it before, like appeals and issues with an earlier trial. The rest would go to Judge Henderson, who would decide which of the other judges to assign each one to. Of course, he would also decide which ones he wanted to keep for himself. A lot would depend on his schedule and the schedules of the other judges."

"So that doesn't tell us much," I say. "It could be a case that would automatically go to our judge, or one that the blackmailers would insist he keep for himself."

"Right. We need to tell the Judge to give us whatever information he already has in that regard."

"That could be a problem; he may view it as confidential. You'd better be the one to ask him."

"Why me?" she asks.

"You're more persuasive and less abrasive than I am."

She doesn't argue the point, so she obviously agrees. "Okay, I'll call him. And let's get together with Marcus as soon as we get the court records. Following up on them will give us something to do."

"That's a plan," I say, as a call-waiting signal tells me another call is coming in. I hang up with Laurie and answer it.

The voice is unmistakably Judge Henderson's and I can hear the tension. "Get over here right now."

"What's wrong?"

"I'll tell you when you get here." Click.

I call Laurie back. "Turns out we've got a new plan."

THE JUDGE IS CONSIDERABLY MORE AGITATED THAN THE LAST TIME WE saw him.

He's obviously not a person inclined to make small talk, but this time he takes that to a new level and says nothing at all in greeting. He leads us into the den, and we're not even seated when he comes over to us with another piece of paper. "I got this in the mail."

"Put it on the table," Laurie tells him.

"What?"

"In case there are fingerprints on it. We don't want to touch it unless we have to."

Henderson nods and places it down. "I'm afraid I've held it without being careful."

"You had no way of knowing what it was," I say.

It's a photograph of the Judge standing in an open doorway, kissing or being kissed by a woman who is probably forty years his junior. He is wearing what appear to be pajamas; she is decked out in a short skirt and a fairly revealing top. Without knowing all the circumstances, we can say with certainty that she has not arrived there straight from her job as a librarian.

The obvious perception from the photograph is that he opened the door to greet her, and they kissed.

The printed letters below the photo read, "Remember Eva Staley?"

"Tell us the circumstances," Laurie says, "please."

"It was a while back; at least a year and a half. I was at a judicial conference in Manhattan, staying at the Marriott Marquis in Times Square; that's where the conference was held. There was a knock on my door one night after I got back from dinner, maybe ten P.M.

"It was a young woman." He points to the photo. "No doubt that young woman, though I don't remember what she looked like. She gave me a big smile and said something like 'Welcome home.' I can't recall exactly . . . I was quite surprised. But it was something to that effect. Then before I realized what was happening, she kissed me."

"What did you do?" I ask.

"Nothing. She immediately said that she was sorry, that she thought I was someone else, and she left. I closed the door and never thought about it again until today when this arrived."

"Did you see anyone else?" Laurie asks.

"No."

"Someone took that picture," I say.

"Obviously. The entire thing was orchestrated. I am expecting you to tell me why."

"At least part of the why is obvious. You are being blackmailed with incriminating information that has been carefully and expensively staged over a long period of time. We will learn what you are being asked to do fairly soon; I'm confident of that. At this point the more important question is who?"

"And what have you learned so far?"

Maybe it's because I'm not used to having a client, but this guy is pissing me off. He seems to think we're lawyers in his courtroom and that we have to kiss his ass. "In the two days we have been on the case," I say, "we haven't learned a thing. Nothing at all. Zero."

"Perhaps you were the wrong choice for this assignment."

"Not too late for you to change your mind." I look at Laurie when I say this. I realize that I'm part of a team and that I'm speaking for more than myself. Fortunately, she nods her support to me.

"I'll take that under advisement," Henderson says. "In the meantime I suggest you go do the job for which you are being paid."

Laurie and I leave, taking the photograph and message with us. We wait until we're in the car to discuss what has just transpired. "That is one annoying guy," I say.

"He's scared but would never show it."

"Even so, I shouldn't have threatened to quit without discussing it with you first."

"Don't worry about it; it was good that you set that boundary." Then, "Whatever is going on, there has been a remarkable amount of advance planning for it. We are up against patient people."

I nod. "Rich, patient people."

"At least we have someone to look for now. Eva Staley. If that's her name."

"That's her name," I say. "They want us to look for her. They want us to hear what she has to say."

"You think they even know there's an 'us' that's involved?"

I nod again. "Absolutely. I wouldn't be surprised if they have the Judge under surveillance. If they're going to put this much money into something, they wouldn't skimp when it came to accumulating information."

"I can have Marcus check that out; it's a specialty of his. He can also find Ms. Staley; that's still another specialty of his."

I'm not thrilled with this; I don't like to have to depend on someone else when the going gets tough. "Tell him it could be dangerous and to call me if he needs help."

"I will. But of all his specialties, handling himself in dangerous situations is absolutely number one."

AS I EXPECTED, EVA STALEY WAS EASY TO FIND.

Laurie tells me that Marcus has learned where she is and what she does for a living. She works on the streets of Paterson, and her career path is hooker. Just perfect for Judge Henderson to greet in his hotel room.

That she is from Paterson is interesting. Her meeting with the Judge was in a Manhattan hotel. I have to assume Manhattan has enough of its own hookers to cover the Times Square hotels, and Eva didn't just accidentally wander into their territory. She was brought there specifically to get the photograph with the Judge.

None of this is surprising, but rather just further evidence of the remarkable planning that went into this effort. I suspect we're going to be finding out the motive soon; there is no reason for the blackmailers to do all this now if they are not about to drop the bomb.

We decide that Marcus and I will question Eva Staley. Laurie wants to go as well, but that would be overkill. All three of us are the type who want to do everything ourselves, but we'll be most effective as a team if we learn to divide up the work.

This will give me a chance to get Simon out of the house and back into at least some semblance of action. He's been uncharacteristically quiet and sort of lazy lately, which I consider understandable. He was an active police dog for seven years, and now all of a sudden he's out of a job with nothing to do. He doesn't have any hobbies, although he likes to chew on sticks.

Marcus picks me up at 10:00 P.M. I hadn't told him about my bringing Simon but he doesn't seem concerned and doesn't say anything when Simon jumps into the backseat. Marcus is not big on saying stuff.

We drive to downtown Paterson. All the retail stores are closed at this hour; Paterson is not to be confused with Manhattan. But the bars are open, and the street we stop on has four of them. We park in front of a fairly large outdoor parking lot, which is also closed, and which at this point has more humans in it than cars.

About a dozen people seem to be in the lot, and they can roughly be divided into two groups: women of the evening, and men who want to spend at least part of the evening with them. There are also one or two men who couldn't more obviously be pimps if they were wearing sandwich boards that said I'M A PIMP AND PROUD OF IT.

It's a depressing scene.

Marcus motions with his head toward the parking lot and says what sounds like "Blrrr." I'm sure that's not the actual word or words he planned to use, but it doesn't matter; I know what he means. Eva Staley is in this parking lot.

We get out of the car and walk into the lot. We immediately attract attention and stares, most likely because of Simon. Not too many johns bring their German shepherds with them when they are looking for retail sex.

Another nod from Marcus tells me which one Eva Staley is, and in the dim light I think I recognize her from her photo in the hotel. I'm not sure how Marcus knew how to identify her, or where she would be, but I don't dwell on it. According to Laurie, Marcus has ways that are not often capable of being understood.

We walk over to Eva, and I say, "Eva Staley?" She turns to see me, but gets momentarily frightened when she sees Simon.

"It's okay, he's harmless, unless I tell him not to be. He won't hurt you. Now, are you Eva Staley?"

"Who wants to know?"

"I'll take that as a yes." Up close like this, a program is not necessary to identify the players. The half dozen women are of varying age and size, but all with similar dress. The two pimps, standing off to the side, supervise. At the moment the three customers are all staring at Simon and preparing to melt away.

They don't know who we are or what to make of us, and uncertainty is not conducive to productive sexual shopping.

"We want to talk to you about the time you met a man in a hotel in Times Square. You knocked on his door, you kissed him, and you posed for a picture."

At first she looks confused. "I don't know what . . ." Then a light goes on. "Oh, yeah . . . I remember. But I didn't pose for no picture."

"What was the man's name?"

"Who are you?"

"I'm the one asking you the questions. What was the man's name?"

"He was a judge. He told me his name, but I don't remember it. But I'd know him if I saw him."

One of the pimps comes over. "What's going on here? They bothering you, Eva?"

Simon growls at his approach; he always could tell the good guys from the bad guys. The pimp stops in his tracks, even though I'm sure his original intent had been to come closer and impose his will on whatever situation was developing. "What is that dog doing here? Who the hell are you?"

"It's okay, Rico. They here asking me about a guy. In New York." Eva added the last part pointedly, as if Rico would understand what she meant.

Even though it's a violation of the Pimpian Code to allow one of his employees to engage in a conversation with men that does not involve money, Rico suddenly seems strangely sanguine about this one. He looks us over, as if judging us, then nods his assent. "Make it quick."

"See you later, Rico. Come back anytime," I say. Then, to Eva, "Why were you there that night?"

"Some guy picked me up and took me there."

"Who was the guy?"

"I don't know, but he was rich, I can tell you that."

"How do you know?"

"He paid me three thousand dollars."

"Why would he do that?"

She shrugs. "I'm not sure. All I know is he said the guy in the hotel had done him a big favor, and he was paying him back. He said I was the guy's type, so sending me was one of the ways he was paying him back. Whatever . . . you know?"

Suddenly there is a noise, then a woman's scream of pain and some fear. I look over and it appears that the non-Rico pimp has hit one of the women across the face, for some unknown transgression.

Marcus has been standing silently next to me, then suddenly

he is not. I swear I never saw or heard him move, but all of a sudden he is not here. He's standing in the pimp section.

He has his hands on the non-Rico pimp and does something I've never seen before. I wish I were watching it on television, so I could DVR it and run it back a few times.

Marcus looks like he is going to slam the guy into the car that he's been standing against, but that's not what he does. Instead he lifts him off his feet and tosses him up and over the car. The guy clears the top of the car by at least eighteen inches; his ass faces the ground as he sails backward, as if he is an Olympic high jumper.

In an ordinary circumstance, if such a thing were possible in this situation, the non-Rico pimp would land on the ground on the other side of the car. That doesn't happen here because the car is parked against a building's brick wall. So the flying pimp instead crashes into the wall and bounces back onto the top of the car, where he lies prone and silent. Rico, apparently lacking pimp team spirit, chooses not to intervene.

"Holy shit," Eva says, and I suspect it's the first accurate thing she's said since we got here.

Trying to get this back on track, I ask Eva if she remembers anything about the guy who set the whole thing up.

"Nope."

"Was he the one who took the picture?"

"I told you, I don't know anything about a picture."

"So you just kissed the guy in the hotel room and left?"

"Are you kidding? I was there all night. You know, I never told anybody about this, but I would. For money, I mean."

"Maybe you should be really careful who you are dealing with, Eva. Whoever is really paying you is dangerous and doesn't care about you."

"I can handle myself. Been doing it long enough."

"Good luck with that."

I signal to Marcus, who has been watching the non-Rico pimp remain still on top of the car. Marcus nods, and then he, Simon, and I get back into the car to leave.

"SHE WAS OBVIOUSLY PART OF THE SETUP," I TELL LAURIE.

Marcus and I have come back to her house to fill her in on the evening developments.

"She wasn't surprised to see us and was prepped on what to say. She almost immediately knew what I was asking about, and believe me, she has had enough encounters with men for that one not to have been top of mind. Even her pimp was in on it."

"He didn't cause you any trouble?"

I shake my head. "No, backed off immediately when he realized who we were. Another pimp caused a bit of a problem, not related to us, but Marcus successfully dealt with him."

"I can imagine," Laurie says.

Marcus just sits silently, not even blushing.

"Eva Staley will come forward if they tell her to and tell whatever story they want her to tell about Judge Henderson. And she'll have the picture to prove it."

"She might have a tough time explaining why someone was there to snap the shot," Laurie says.

"Maybe, but that won't matter. The public wouldn't be looking for nuance; they'd latch on to the scandal and the damage to the Judge's reputation would already be done."

She nods. "And all of this, Eva Staley and the Caymans account, were all done more than a year in advance by people who knew what they would want and when they would want it."

"You think they're done? Do they have more bullets to fire?"

"They might," she says. "But anything after this would be overkill. If the Judge was going to do what they ask, this would already be enough to persuade him."

"I'm thinking that Eva Staley is not about scaring Henderson with a sex scandal. First of all, he's not married." The Judge was widowed a few years ago. "Does he have any family?"

"Andy said he thinks he has a son in California, but didn't know any more than that. But hiring a prostitute would be a disaster for the Judge's reputation, married or not."

I nod. "True, but that's not the main reason I don't think this is about a sex scandal, or even about prostitution. Eva Staley said that somebody paid her a lot of money and sent her to Henderson to partially repay a favor. The Caymans money would account for the rest of the payback. They are going to claim that the Judge already did something illegal. That's what they're threatening him with."

Laurie nods. "Which is why we have to get those court records. Marcus, you'll have them tomorrow?"

"Yunnh."

"Good. Because if they're claiming that the Judge fixed a case for them, we have an approximate time frame based on when the money started flowing into the Caymans, and when Eva Staley went to the Judge's hotel room."

"She didn't provide a date," I say.

"That's okay; the Judge's calendar will show when he was at the conference in NY. So we'll know when, and we also can make a good guess as to the type of defendant they will claim the Judge helped. He or she would have been wealthy, so as to be able to provide the money for the Caymans account."

"You want to contact the Judge to find out when he was at the conference?"

Laurie nods. "I will. I'll also tell him about your conversation with Eva Staley. He has a right to know what he's up against."

"It might be time to bring the police into this."

"I don't think so. They haven't made a demand yet, and without that there can't be a blackmail charge. Plus he knows that once he brings them in, there's no guarantee the whole thing won't go public. But it will obviously be up to him; he knows what he's doing."

"He thinks he knows what he's doing, but he doesn't," I say. "He thinks he can control this like he controls the lawyers in his courtroom, but the people he's dealing with aren't the type to rise respectfully when he walks into a room."

"That's why he has us."

There isn't anything more to be said; we're still in the dark. Starting tomorrow we can dig into the court records and try to identify the relevant players who have appeared before Henderson, or who might be coming up in the future.

Marcus must have left, though I didn't see him go. One minute he's in a place and the next he's gone. For a guy whose presence is frightening and dominating, he has an amazing ability to get around without being noticed.

"Where's Marcus?" I ask.

"He must have gone. He'll be back tomorrow with the court records."

"I've never seen anything like how he dealt with that pimp. He was no small guy; must have been close to two hundred pounds. Marcus picked him up and launched him over a car, like the guy was made of straw."

Laurie nods. "It took me a while, but you'll get used to it too." Then, "There is Marcus and then there is everybody else."

MARCUS GOT THE CALL THAT THE COURT RECORDS WERE READY TO BE picked up.

It presented a dilemma, even though he was currently at the courthouse. That morning, Marcus had been at Judge Henderson's house and watched as he left for work. Marcus also watched as a man in a dark green Ford Fusion followed the Judge.

Marcus had gone to the Judge's house in the first place to see if the Judge was being surveilled. Both Corey and Laurie had considered it a distinct possibility; if someone was threatening to blackmail the Judge, they would want to know whom the Judge was aligning himself with, especially if it was the police.

Marcus made a mental note to recommend that the Judge's house be swept for listening devices and phone taps; it would be the logical thing for the blackmailers to do.

Marcus did not follow too closely; he knew where the Judge was going, so therefore he knew where the person tailing him was going. Marcus took down the license plate, then when he arrived downtown, located the car parked near the courtroom. From that spot the blackmailer would be able to see the Judge's car in the employee parking lot, so it would be easy to follow him wherever he was going when the court day was over.

The call saying the records were available came at four thirty in the afternoon, and therein was the dilemma. Marcus knew that if he went in to get them, he might miss the Judge and the guy following him. If he didn't go in, then it would be another wasted day without access to the records.

There was no time to call his partners to tell them to get the records; the court day would be over by the time they arrived. So Marcus called Laurie, told her what was happening, and gave her the license plate number to run. She didn't think it was urgent enough to try to call the Judge while he was in court, so she just told Marcus he should get the records, which he did.

Sure enough, the Judge and the guy tailing him were gone by the time Marcus got back. That was okay. He had no reason to think the Judge was in any danger; if Marcus did, he wouldn't have risked missing him. There would be no reason for a blackmailer to harm the intended victim; the opposite was true. If the blackmailers hoped to get anything out of the Judge, they needed him alive, healthy, and working.

So if Marcus wanted to, he could resume his own surveillance tomorrow. By then he would know who had the Judge in his sights.

I CALL IN ANOTHER FAVOR FROM A FRIEND ON THE FORCE.

This time it's to ask Joey Iurato to run the license plate on the car that Marcus followed this morning. I'm going to have to take each of these guys that helps me out for a night of drinking, and I'll have to pick up the tab. At this rate I will be a penniless alcoholic by the end of the month.

I'm not surprised when it takes just a few minutes for Joey to run the plate and get back to me, but I am surprised by the results. The car is registered to Kevin Vickers, and I know him.

Vickers started out as a cop in the Clifton Police Department, but left after a couple of years to go into private practice. I had heard that it did not go well, that clients were few and far between. Vickers moved into other areas, like working for bail bondsmen, but remained on the fringe of the legal and investigative community.

I knew Vickers because I dated one of his sister's close friends in high school. She was great looking and fun and smart, so of course I avoided any chance of a future with her.

As I recall, Vickers was not exactly a model citizen or student in high school, and I remember being surprised that he became a cop. I didn't know him well back in those days and I was fine with that.

Joey has gone above and beyond and provided me with Vickers's rap sheet; I hadn't realized he even had one. There was an arrest for assault and one for passing a bad check, both in the years after he left the force. None of them went to trial; the assault charge somehow went away, and he pleaded no contest to the check issue.

He got off with community service. It doesn't show whether he performed it, but it seems to have been resolved.

We're meeting at Laurie's house tonight, and as we arrive, she has just put her ten-year-old son, Ricky, to bed. Laurie wanted to meet here since we might want to call on Andy to help explain the court records. It's delayed some since Ricky wants to spend a little time with his "Uncle Marcus."

Before we look at the records, we discuss Vickers, and what we should do about him. Everyone agrees that we should not approach him in any fashion; there is no sense at this point in letting him know we are aware of his involvement.

"I don't think he's a danger to the Judge," I say. "He's a scumbag, but I doubt that murder is part of his résumé. Also, they would have no reason to physically harm the Judge at this point; not while they think he can be useful. With all the trouble they went to in order to frame him, he's much more potentially valuable alive and well."

"I agree," says Laurie, and Marcus nods his assent.

"Do you think the Judge could have hired him as well as us?" Laurie asks. "Maybe for protection?"

"I doubt it. They inhabit different worlds. But we need to tell him about this. Even though we don't think he's in any imminent danger, we could be wrong. If someone was following me, I'd want to know about it."

Laurie nods. "Agreed. I'll tell him." Then, "You guys hungry?"

As Marcus and I answer yes, Andy walks into the room. "How are my favorite employees doing? Any ass-kissing compliments you want to pay the boss, in this case, me?"

"Your favorite employees are hungry," Laurie says. "Pizza would be nice."

Andy nods. "Pizza is always nice. It's pretty hard to hate a pizza."

"Would the boss be willing to go pick some up?" Laurie asks. "I mean, since he's the only one without any actual work to do."

He agrees after sneering and moaning for a bit, and we all tell him the toppings we want on our pizzas. He's heading down to pick them up at Patsy's, that rare New Jersey restaurant that can match New York pizza slice for slice.

With that accomplished, we dive into the court records for cases Judge Henderson presided over starting six months before the first deposit was made into the Caymans account. Laurie had learned that the conference Judge Henderson attended was also in that same general time frame.

The six months is an arbitrary figure, but seems comfortable. It is unlikely that the bad guys would have waited longer than that if they had information that was valuable and could lead to something they wanted down the road. If we need to, we can go back and start earlier.

We've got two significant problems with this process. One is that we don't even know what we are looking for. Our supposition, which certainly could be wrong, is that the blackmailers are prepared to claim that Judge Henderson already acted improperly on one of these cases, and that they will threaten to reveal it.

They will point to the Caymans account and Eva Staley as a payoff for his having done that improper deed. But to make it stick, they'd have to have credible evidence that he actually did something wrong. We hope to find it in these records, even though I think we all doubt that he actually did what they will claim.

Our other problem is that we don't have enough expertise to capably analyze what we're looking at. We've divvied up the trial transcripts and we're each about three pages in before we come to this unfortunate realization.

"This is lawyer's work," I say.

Laurie nods. "Maybe I shouldn't have sent our lawyer out for pizza. On the other hand, we're really hungry, and pizza is pizza."

When Andy comes back, we chow down. Laurie's mouth is still full as she tells Andy the problem we are having. She's not even a third of the way through when he says, "I don't like where this is going."

"I suspected you'd have reservations. I hope that your love for me will allow you to overcome them."

"You want me to read through all these transcripts in the hope of finding something that likely isn't there?" He sounds incredulous at the prospect. "And I should do it for love?"

"That sums it up."

"Another love I have is not working. And the one thing Hatchet and I agreed on was that neither of us wanted me involved."

I continue not to say anything; this is best handled by Laurie, and I think she's closing in for the kill. "These are extraordinary circumstances," she says.

"This is not my idea of a restful retirement. And how much is the K Team prepared to pay me for this work?"

"You're doing it pro bono because that's the kind of guy you are. You're my hero."

WE RECONVENE AT LAURIE AND ANDY'S AT 2:00 P.M. TO HEAR WHAT ANDY has learned.

I'm surprised that Andy has gone through all of the documents so quickly; maybe he just wanted to get it over with, or maybe he just did a cursory job. He seems unlikely to be voted Man of the Year by *Work Ethic Magazine*.

Marcus is not here; he feels his time is better spent keeping an eye on Vickers, who in turn is following the Judge. Laurie has told the Judge about Vickers, and the Judge was upset about it. I can't say that I blame him.

He reluctantly agreed that we should not intervene, at least for the moment. Vickers is not technically doing anything illegal, and he doesn't seem to represent a physical danger to the Judge. If that seems about to change, Marcus will be there. I know Vickers to be a tough guy, but he is not Marcus. The Russian army is not Marcus.

I've brought Simon with me since this house is obviously dog friendly. Simon and Tara seem to like each other. Andy and Laurie's other dog, a basset named Sebastian, doesn't seem terribly interested in either of them. He seems most interested in sleeping.

Once we're settled in, Andy begins telling us what he's learned. "First, I need to preface all this by placing it in overall context.

"A judge handles many things besides trials. He or she hears motions, holds discovery hearings, status conferences, plea bargains, signs off on search warrants, and much more. These could take place between trials or even during trials.

"So that makes what we are trying to find that much more difficult. Hatchet, or any judge, can issue rulings that have major real-world significance, and those decisions can essentially be mostly under the radar.

"The other thing I want to say is I consider Hatchet to be obnoxious, dictatorial, arrogant, pompous, and inconsiderate. I do not consider him corrupt. I don't think we will find unethical behavior because I don't believe he would act unethically. And it is inconceivable to me that he would accept any kind of bribe or payoff. That is not who he is.

"But he has two other good qualities. He's very smart. I cannot imagine him acting in a way that would put him in this position. He is a target in this situation, not a conspirator."

"What's the other good quality?"

"Take him out of his job, get a few drinks in him, and he can be a hell of a lot of fun. I was sitting next to him at a charity dinner once; when I saw him there, I almost bailed out of the dinner. But he had two glasses of wine, and he opened up. He and I were the only two people in the entire place not wearing ties. He told me he never does, that he hates ties and shoes. He says he insists on his neck and feet having room to breathe."

I can't help smiling at Andy's recounting of that night. If I drew the short straw and had to sit next to Henderson at a stuffy charity dinner, I'd be miserable. Just being at a stuffy charity dinner would be enough to make my head explode.

"I noticed he doesn't wear ties in court," Laurie says, "the only judge I ever saw that doesn't."

Andy nods. "And I'll bet he's wearing flip-flops under those long robes. But getting back to the point, the guy is honest. I'd bet on it."

"Understood," I say, and Laurie nods her agreement. I've never heard any reason to think the Judge is anything less than honest, but to hear it from somebody like Andy, who has tried cases before him and who clearly cannot stand him, is significant.

Andy continues, "So, in the six-month period that we are talking about, Hatchet conducted eight trials. He also presided over many other matters, like the ones I described. I could go over everything with you or just tell you the ones that might conceivably hold some promise."

Laurie and I both opt for the latter. If Andy doesn't think anything significant is in the other stuff, we are not likely to either. Besides, we can always come back and revisit it if we think we need to.

"Okay. Let's start with the trials," Andy says. "Three or four of them are what I would consider nonprospects, so let's get them out of the way first. "Two were for relatively low-level drug offenses. One was breaking and entering, and the other was intentional manslaughter, the result of a bar fight."

"You listed four, but you said that three or four were nonprospects," Laurie says. "Which one are you unsure of?"

"The bar fight. The other three were trials in which the defendants had significant criminal records, but all low-level stuff. They had very little money and were represented by the public defender. Whatever is going on in our case, there is certainly significant money involved."

"How was the bar fight different?" I ask.

"The defendant"—Andy looks at a document—"John Lowry . . . basically had no criminal record at all. He also was an apparently productive member of the labor force. He worked as an IT computer guy, the company he worked for would send him out as a troubleshooter to large corporations. Then he took a job in the financial industry.

"But he wasn't wealthy, and the thing that stands out is that he was represented by Walter Cummings. That surprised me."

I know Cummings; I once tangled with him when I testified in a murder case. He is top-of-the-line, in ability but especially in price. He does not work cheap.

Andy continues, "But there isn't much in the transcript to indicate that Hatchet did anything unusual or controversial. I was a little surprised by his charge to the jury, but it wasn't out of bounds, and the guy was convicted. Lowry killed the guy with one punch, and Cummings tried self-defense. But a witness says the punch Lowry threw was the only one.

"Most of Cummings's efforts seemed designed to get his client a soft sentence; including stressing the fact that Lowry was helping a woman whom the victim had just mistreated. It didn't work; Lowry received ten years, which seems in line with the guidelines."

Andy moves along to the cases that hold more promise. "One is an embezzlement case; a woman named Nina Williams was alleged to have stolen one hundred thousand dollars from a grocery-supply company here in Paterson. She had worked in their accounts receivable department. Hatchet made a ruling in that case that certain evidence found in her apartment was incorrectly obtained, making it inadmissible. I'm not sure I agree with his ruling, but because of it she ultimately went free.

"Another was a murder trial of a known organized-crime figure in Paterson. His name is Gerry Infante, a tough guy who weighs close to three hundred pounds. His nickname is Big Gerry, which among his other faults shows a lack of nickname creativity. He was a lieutenant in the Petrone/Russo crime family, which disbanded due to the untimely deaths of both Petrone and Russo.

"Infante was accused of strangling his fiancée, Cynthia Goffin, after discovering her cheating on him. In addition to screwing up his wedding plans, he was convicted in Hatchet's court and sentenced to twenty-five years to life. I don't see any questionable decisions by Hatchet here; I am including it because of the organized-crime connection. They are the types who would have no qualms of conscience about blackmailing a judge and would have access to the necessary funds to do it.

"Last is Drew Lockman, who stood accused of fraud. He was a partner in a brokerage, running a Ponzi scheme, sort of a reduced version of Madoff. He took about four million dollars of investors' money, after convincing them he was some kind of investment savant.

"Didn't take long for the money to be gone, but Lockman apparently lived quite well in the process. The people who invested with him should have been brought up on stupidity charges. He invested the cash in businesses that had a tendency to benefit him and his family, most of which went under.

"He wound up with an acquittal because the prosecution couldn't prove that he didn't just legitimately lose the money and that the living well wasn't necessary to travel in that world and network successfully for his clients. Hatchet's charge to the jury surprised me; he made it fairly obvious that he did not believe the prosecution had proven guilt beyond a reasonable doubt.

"The jury agreed and deliberated less than six hours before letting him go. What they would have done without Hatchet's charge to them, I have no way of knowing, but given the evidence, I don't think they made a mistake.

"There's one other thing I should point out: judges make rulings all the time that are close calls. It would be easy for anyone to say that Hatchet ruled a certain way because he was paid off. The Caymans account and Eva Staley would tend to support their position, even if they are lying through their teeth."

"Understood. So bottom line," I say, "which case holds the most promise?"

Andy thinks for a few moments, then: "None of them."

MARIA BURKS WAS A PRETTY ACCURATE SELF-EVALUATOR.

She knew what she was good at, and where she was deficient.

For example, she could make her own clothes, and no one would ever know they weren't store-bought. She was so handy that she could fix pretty much anything in her apartment; she had learned all of that from watching her father back in the day. It was necessary since on their income there was no such thing as hiring a professional handyman. And she could remember stuff; if her memory wasn't what they called photographic, it was damn close.

On the other side of the ledger, she could never understand finance, which was not a big problem because she never had any money. She couldn't cook a thing, but that helped her keep her weight down. And she didn't have even a trace of a sense of humor; when it came to telling a joke or getting one, Maria was lost. She was forced to pretend, which was not easy. When someone told her a joke, she struggled to figure out the correct time to fake laugh.

But the one thing she was absolutely the worst at was picking men, which is why she had basically decided to stop trying. Every man she had ever dated for any length of time either abused her or demeaned her. For a while she was hoping to find one who simply ignored her, but she eventually gave up the hunt.

So Maria had accepted it as a fact of life and hadn't had a date in three months. She had turned down a couple of men who seemed nice on the surface, since she no longer had any desire to watch as their true colors eventually came out.

She had also decided to move out of New Jersey, in an effort to start fresh. She moved to Dayton, Ohio, where an old high school friend lived. And things had worked out quite well. She made a bunch more friends and got a decent job at the Dayton Walmart.

In truth, Maria didn't miss dating at all. Her new lifestyle made getting up for work a lot easier. No more late nights in bars, drinking too much and dropping into bed in the early hours of the morning. When Maria woke up now, she was clearheaded and had energy. That took some getting used to.

This day was a perfect example. She woke up at six, put on a T-shirt and sweatpants, and went for a two-mile run. Then she came back, took a shower, and dressed for work.

Once that was accomplished, she walked out to the detached garage that she shared with her upstairs neighbor. She got into the car without realizing a man was in the backseat.

Not until she felt his hands on her neck did she know of his presence.

By then it was too late.

MY FATHER WAS RATHER SET IN HIS VERBAL WAYS.

Actually, he was set in all his ways. He wanted the things in his control done the right way, and he wanted to control everything. I was one of the items he had control over, and he exercised it until I summoned the courage to claim adulthood.

Roger Douglas was a cop, a sergeant in the Paterson Police Department. He sustained a devastating injury after twenty years on the job when conducting a routine traffic stop on Route 20. A drunk driver passing by swerved too close and hit him.

He wound up with bones that he hadn't even known he had being broken and was never the same. He had to retire, which I believe did what the drunk driver could not. It killed him.

But getting back to his verbal demands, he had ways to describe things and ways not to describe them. For example, he would never abide anyone referring to conducting investigations as doing "legwork." Most of his colleagues used that word as a positive, a sign of doing one's job diligently and thoroughly.

Not my dad.

He considered it demeaning; he felt that the legs were not nearly the most important body parts in the investigative process. The mind was, of course, first. Trailing behind was the mouth, for knowing the right questions to ask. Even more important were the ears. The ability to truly listen was everything.

But with apologies to Dad if he is looking down, I would describe what Laurie, Marcus, and I are doing as legwork. We are dividing up the cases that Andy described, along with a few others he didn't deem worthy, and looking into them.

Today I am looking for Kenny Chandler, who had what could be called a direct connection to one of the cases Hatchet presided over within the time frame we are looking at. Kenny was having an affair with Cynthia Goffin, who was engaged to Gerry "Big Gerry" Infante.

It was not the best choice Kenny could have made, and that's not a reflection on Cynthia's attractiveness or appeal. Infante frowned on his fiancée fooling around, and since he was a three-hundred-pound lieutenant in the Petrone/Russo crime family, his frown was of some significance.

Infante retaliated by strangling Cynthia, after which he went hunting for Kenny. While Kenny's ability to choose safe and productive relationships left something to be desired, his self-preservation instinct was functioning quite well. He went into hiding and didn't come out until well after the police had arrested Infante for Cynthia's murder.

Hatchet presided over Infante's trial, which ended in his conviction and his being sent away for most if not all of the rest of his life. Kenny did not have to testify at trial and his name was not even mentioned because the evidence was sufficient to convict Infante, so the prosecution apparently did not feel the need to get heavily into motive.

In New Jersey, as in every other state in the union, murdering one's fiancé or fiancée is illegal even if he or she has done something really annoying. Still, since the prosecution had motive evidence, mainly the affair that the victim was having with Kenny, I would have thought they would have used it.

Kenny's own rap sheet indicates that he himself would not likely be described as either a sportsman or a scholar. He has three arrests and one conviction on drug charges, selling and not using, but has so far avoided jail time. My former colleagues on the drug side think it's only a matter of time before his luck runs out.

Kenny works out of a storefront office in Paterson, though he is out and about most of the day. He must be an outdoorsman because he spends a good deal of his time in Pennington Park, hanging out with friends and likely meeting up with customers.

So Simon and I head out to spend some time in the park. I don't bring any toys or tennis balls for Simon to play with; if he needs to chew on anything, he can use Kenny's leg.

Kenny has set up shop near the home plate batting cage on the baseball field. I recognize him from his mug shot, but he would be easy to pick out. He's in a small group of six people and seems to be the center of attention. It's hard to know if the other people are buyers or co-sellers, but the body language and position of Kenny and the others indicate that Kenny is at least the leader among a pathetic band of equals.

I park the car and put a leash on Simon. We start walking directly toward the group, at first attracting little attention. It is just not unusual for someone to be out walking his dog in the park, even a dog as spectacular as Simon.

We're about fifty feet away when they realize that we are heading directly and purposefully toward them. I'm sure most, if not all, of them are thinking, *Cop*. They start to melt away, leaving Kenny alone. Kenny doesn't melt, probably as a demonstration of his toughness and authority.

This is his turf.

"Hello, Kenny."

"You're a cop," he says, dispensing with a hello.

I've thought about this. I have enough leftover ID to pass as a current police officer, and it could certainly help in some investigations for people to think so. But I'm not going to actively deceive in that manner; it doesn't feel right. I retired, so if there are perks to being active, I'm not entitled to them.

But in this case Kenny has made the assessment and I am under no obligation to correct him. So I neither confirm nor deny; he can think whatever he wants.

Simon moves close to Kenny and sits up straight, making a noise and sitting upright, both of which mean he is onto something. It's intimidating to Kenny, as it would be to pretty much everyone this side of Marcus, and Kenny says, "What's with your dog?"

"He believes you have some illegal drugs in your possession. He's really good at this."

"No way, man."

"The good news for you is that right now I'm not interested in drugs. I'm here to talk. If you'd rather not talk, I can adjust my interest."

He doesn't look convinced, even though I used my sincere voice. But he asks, "Talk about what?"

"Gerry Infante's trial."

The extent of worry on his face instantly doubles. "What about it? That's history, man."

"Why didn't you testify?"

"I didn't want to, and I guess my lawyer took care of it. I wanted to stay as far away from that as I could. Infante is bad news."

"Did your lawyer say how he took care of it?"

Kenny shakes his head. "Nah. And I didn't ask. All I know is, it worked out."

"Who was your lawyer?"

"A guy named Gutierrez. Carlos Gutierrez. Smart guy; he earned his money."

I don't have much more to ask Kenny; this little outing in the park was just to make an assessment of him. I'll look up Gutierrez, who no doubt knows more about the trial than Kenny does. The fence Kenny is standing against knows more about it than he does.

"Have any of Infante's friends come after you?" I ask.

"No. You think they will?"

"Absolutely. Those guys never forget."

"I can handle myself," he says with no confidence at all.

"No, you can't."

Simon and I leave, and I call one of my ex-colleagues to report my certainty that Kenny is in the park, carrying and selling drugs.

With any luck, he'll wind up in a cell with Gerry Infante.

JUDGE HENDERSON WANTED, EVEN NEEDED, SOMEONE TO TALK TO.

Just realizing that surprised him a bit and embarrassed him even more. He always prided himself on wanting or needing little besides what he already had; it was a way he maintained control. Control over others, over his environment, over himself.

But this situation worried him deeply. Even baseless accusations, if sensational enough, could ruin reputations and lives. That had always been the case, but never more so than in this new world of social media and a public seemingly thirsting for the next gotcha.

Lies make the front page, Henderson knew, while retractions are buried on the bottom of page 38. And if any occupation was more dependent on a spotless reputation, it would have to be a judge's.

He had few people to talk to. Judge Henderson had worries and insecurities like anyone else; he was just never big in confiding in anyone. And this situation was even more delicate because it had to be held in the strictest confidence by anyone he spoke with.

So the Judge had no list of confidants to pick from, but if there had been, the two names at the top would have been Judge Robert Pletka and Peter Tuckman.

Judge Pletka was essentially second-in-command in the Passaic County court system. He started out as a prosecutor and then moved into a judgeship at age thirty-seven.

From day one he showed proper deference and respect to Judge Henderson, so Judge Henderson took him under his wing. If Henderson could be said to have a protégé, it would be Judge Pletka. They shared the same judicial philosophy and the same reverence for the law and proper procedure. Both men were reviled by attorneys who practiced before them, but those same attorneys almost unanimously recognized the evenhandedness and ability of the two judges.

Over time they'd established a personal rapport as well. Judge Pletka had spoken with his friend about his own problems. His wife had a progressive lung disease that was difficult to treat and occasionally debilitating. There was little doubt that they would eventually have to move to a dry, more favorable climate; Arizona was the logical choice.

But it would be difficult for Pletka to give up his job and essentially start over, especially since on a Passaic County judge's salary he had not put much away. Judge Henderson had listened and advised and offered to help in any way he could.

Peter Tuckman, the other member of the Henderson consultation team, was the head of public relations for the Passaic County court system. As chief judge, Henderson had come to rely on Tuckman whenever something controversial involving the courts had come up. Henderson had insisted on Tuckman's presence because his specialty was damage control, and in this case there was no shortage of damage to control.

Tuckman was smart, savvy in the areas that Judge Henderson was not. Tuckman had almost unfailingly given the Judge good advice in the past, so he was an obvious choice to consult in this situation.

So Henderson invited Judge Pletka and Tuckman to lunch in his chambers and unburdened himself. He told them about the threats, about the faked evidence, and about his hiring investigators to help him deal with all of it.

When he was finished, Pletka asked, "And you don't know what they are going to claim?"

Henderson shook his head. "No, and I've thought about it. I mean, you know all too well that in any trial there are countless decisions that we make, and some people would consider them wrongly made. But I obviously think every ruling can be defended or I wouldn't have made it in the first place."

Tuckman nodded at the obvious logic. "And no idea what they are going to ask you to do?"

Another shake of the head. "None. And I haven't figured out what to do when the demand is made."

"How do you see your options?"

"I can recuse, but I really hate to do that. It feels like a victory for them, even though that's not what they want. Or I could tell them to go to hell, in which case they'd go public with the Caymans account, and the woman at the hotel."

"Which will mean that all bets are officially off," Pletka said.

Henderson nodded. "Correct. And I'd probably wind up having to recuse from everything while I defended myself anyway."

"Any thought of going to the police?" Tuckman asked

"I've thought about it a lot, but that risks it going public. And I don't see the upside."

"Maybe they can find out who is doing this?"

"I've got good people on it now; I have to let it play out."

Pletka did not seem convinced by that. "You need to worry about your personal safety, Henry."

Henderson nodded. "I know that, especially because of something I didn't mention."

"What's that?"

"I'm being followed. Somebody is watching me, apparently at all times."

"What?" Pletka make no effort to hide his astonishment. "How do you know that?"

"The investigators I hired detected him. We know his name and a great deal about him."

"What are you doing about it?" Tuckman asked.

"For the moment, nothing. The assessment is that he does not represent a danger at this point, and I agree with that. They're not doing electronic surveillance; we had my home checked for bugs and phone taps."

"This is unbelievable."

"It does seem a bit surreal. At some point, probably soon, we'll intervene and question the man who's following me; maybe we'll find a way to arrest him. That way we'll have leverage to get him to reveal his employer."

"You're much calmer about all this than I would be," Pletka said.

"That could change on a dime."

The three men agreed to reconvene regularly to deal with what was obviously going to be a fluid situation.

"Hang in," Tuckman said, "this too shall pass."

NINA WILLIAMS STOLE $105,000.

She would be the first to admit that. She had already admitted it multiple times. But Nina Williams never served a day in jail for her crime and was never even prosecuted.

Nina was a bookkeeper, the head bookkeeper, for a Paterson company called FoodMart, which sold grocery supplies in seven states, obviously including New Jersey. By all accounts she was an excellent bookkeeper, but an even better crook, because she stole the money with an elaborate scam that was never detected.

It still hasn't officially been detected.

Bookkeeping smarts do not necessarily translate to overall life smarts, and Nina was a perfect example of that. One night, when out drinking with a coworker, Michele Winston, Nina drunkenly bragged about her embezzling prowess.

The coworker wasn't quite as drunk as Nina and was also not impressed by Nina's accomplishments. Michele shared it with her manager the first thing the next morning, and Nina's successful crime spree and job came to a quick end.

They determined that the money was missing, but Nina had covered her tracks so well that they couldn't demonstrate conclusively that she was responsible. Taken alone, the drunken comment to Michele Winston would not carry the day in any court of law.

Nina decided she needed a fresh start in a state where she wasn't known to be a crook, so she took her stolen nest egg and moved rather hastily to Maryland, where she had family. She told her landlord that she was leaving and would send for her stuff.

He was not thrilled with that since she was chronically late with her rent and was two weeks overdue on her payment. He was fine losing her as a tenant, but told her he wanted the money he was owed. Nina said she would be sending the money, a promise that experience told him was empty.

When the police finally visited her apartment, the landlord explained the situation. He also told them they were welcome to look at anything they wanted, that he now owned everything because she hadn't paid up.

The police found in her possessions a ledger that incriminated her, and she was arrested. She hired her cousin as her lawyer, and while hiring cousins simply because of their availability and family loyalty might not always be the best idea, in this case it worked out quite well.

The cousin pointed to a clause in the lease saying that she could not be officially evicted until the rent had not been paid for thirty days. Since the police entered the apartment on the twenty-eighth day, he argued that it was still technically her apartment, and that the police had entered without a proper search warrant.

He filed a pretrial motion to have the evidence ruled inadmissible. He also pointed out that if it was tainted, then all the investigating that was done—and all the new evidence that was uncovered—as a result of that evidence having served as a road map should also be disallowed. It was "fruit from the poison tree."

Judge Henderson agreed with Nina's cousin, and his ruling essentially destroyed the prosecution's case. They dismissed the charges.

Nina had absolutely no interest in agreeing to be interviewed by Laurie. Since Nina was never brought to trial, double jeopardy had not attached, so she could still be charged and tried. Therefore, she had learned her lesson and would never say another word about it to anyone.

But her lawyer-cousin, Jeff Springer, had no such reservations. He knew of Laurie and knew she was married to Andy Carpenter; this was Springer's chance to brag.

"You never saw more pissed-off prosecutors than at that hearing," he said, when Laurie brought it up. "Does Andy know about it? 'Cause it didn't exactly get a lot of press."

"I haven't discussed it with Andy." She didn't think it necessary to mention that Andy had gone over all of Judge Henderson's cases.

"You might want to show him the transcript; he'll appreciate it. It was one of those great defense attorney moments; we don't have that many of them."

"Other than the fact that it was one of those moments, was there anything else about the hearing and ruling that surprised you?"

"Why are you interested in this?"

"I really can't say. But it has nothing to do with your client."

He considers that for a moment and finally nods his agreement. "Okay . . . let's see . . . anything that surprised me. Well, Hatchet's . . . that's what we call Judge Henderson, but I can't tell you why . . . anyway, his ruling surprised me some."

"Why?"

"Well, the law was pretty clear; they screwed up with the search of the apartment and it should have killed their case. But I figured Hatchet would find a way around it, that he'd come up with a way to let the evidence in."

"Why?"

"That's the kind of guy he is. It's why defense attorneys hate him." Springer smiles at the memory. "You should have seen his face when he dismissed the charges. It was killing him."

"But you think he acted properly?"

"Oh, yeah. He had no choice or he wouldn't have done it. Even the prosecutors knew it was coming. The appeals court would have smacked him down; no judge likes that."

"Okay. That's all I need to know."

"You really should get the transcript and show it to Andy. He'd get a kick out of it."

TWO LAWYERS FROM TWO DIFFERENT WORLDS.

That's the best way to describe Carlos Gutierrez and Walter Cummings.

I briefly met with Gutierrez this morning. He is the attorney who represented Kenny Chandler, whose major claim to fame is not his drug dealing, but rather his being the third part of the love triangle that resulted in Gerry Infante going to prison.

I met with Gutierrez in his downtown Paterson office. It's one room, which he shares with his assistant, or paralegal, or whatever she is. Charitably put, it's a dump.

Kenny Chandler somehow got out of testifying in the Infante trial, but told me he had no idea how that came about. Gutierrez was quite happy to take the time to talk about the case; I have a feeling he doesn't have clients beating down his door and demanding his attention.

The problem is that he doesn't know why Chandler wasn't

called either. But he certainly sees it as a prosecutorial decision and one that had nothing whatsoever to do with Judge Henderson. Whatever the reason behind the decision, he has no problem with it. "Hey, it worked. They got their conviction, and Infante is away for a very long time."

"So you weren't involved with them in making the decision?"

"No. They told me to keep Kenny available to be called, and then they said forget it. Kenny thinks I had something to do with it, but I didn't."

"He might have a need for you in the future."

He smiles. "Could be. But only if he's careful."

"What do you mean?"

"Infante has a few friends on the outside. I wouldn't want to be the guy starting Kenny's car every morning."

On that happy note, I went to the Ridgewood office of Walter Cummings, a founding partner in Cummings, Hampton & Daniels, which is where I am now. The elevator is the size of Gutierrez's office, and the reception area makes me feel underdressed.

I'm told that this firm does mostly corporate work and handles few criminal cases. Whatever they do, they are obviously well paid for their efforts.

The two receptionists are both young and attractive and both with professional, welcoming smiles. I choose the one on the right, for no particular reason. I have a feeling I could not have gone wrong with either. I tell her that I am here to see Cummings, and after they confirm that I have an appointment, I'm ushered back to his office.

Cummings is probably sixty and has the look for which the word *distinguished* was invented. We chitchat for maybe thirty seconds, but he acts as if in a hurry.

"You wanted to talk about John Lowry? I'm sure you

understand that there is very little I could say without breaching confidentiality."

"He punched someone in a bar at two o'clock in the morning and killed him."

Cummings nods. "I'm aware of the details of the case."

"He doesn't strike me as your typical client."

A slight smile. "Wherever I see wrongs, I attempt to right them."

"How did he manage to pay you for this particular attempt?" Lowry was an IT guy, a troubleshooter, working mostly in the financial sector. He probably made decent money, but decent money wouldn't get it done with Walter Cummings.

"Do you have any questions I can answer? Because if not . . ."

"Was there anything unusual about the trial?"

"In what sense? Each trial is unique."

"Maybe in the prosecution's handling of the case? The Judge's rulings?"

"Why are you asking me this?"

I smile. "Do you have any questions I can answer?"

"Very well. Nothing out of the ordinary comes to mind, other than perhaps the jury's decision. I do not like to lose and fortunately have not had that experience very often. As for the Judge, he made some rulings which I consider to have been in error."

"What were they?"

"They will be in my next court filing; I can only refer you to that."

"Did the jury's verdict surprise you?"

"It disappointed me. I refer you to my comment about not liking to lose. Nor have I come close to giving up. Now, have you got what you've come for? I do have things to attend to."

"I appreciate the time. Thanks."

As I'm getting to my car, my cell phone rings, and I see that it's Laurie.

"What's up?" I ask.

"Judge Henderson called; he got another message. They're starting to set their terms."

"THEY SENT ME A TEXT MESSAGE. THAT IN ITSELF IS EXTREMELY DISCONCERTING," Henderson says.

Laurie and I are meeting with him in his chambers at the courthouse. "You mean because they had your cell phone number?" Laurie asks.

"Exactly. It's my private number. Very few people have it. Now I will have to change it."

I shake my head. "Don't. We want them to be able to contact you. It increases the chance they will make a mistake and reveal themselves." Then, "Let's see the message."

He hands me the phone, I read it, then hand it to Laurie. The message says, "Valdez is coming."

"Any idea what that means?" she asks Henderson.

I don't mention that it is the title of a bad Burt Lancaster movie from the early seventies. I would humbly say that I am one of the world's foremost film-trivia experts; I basically know details about almost every movie of consequence that has ever been released. But this is not the time to reveal my prowess, especially since I don't think Burt is involved with this case.

"I have a trial coming up relatively soon; the defendant is Luis Valdez. The charge is double homicide."

"I know all about Valdez," I say. "I was in on the arrest right before I retired. We trapped him in a warehouse, and Simon located where he was hiding. He wanted no part of Simon."

Laurie nods. "I remember reading about it. He was in the X Gang, right? Chico Simmons?"

Laurie doesn't point out that Chico was himself killed on a drug case that she was working on for one of Andy's clients. It's not on Henderson's need-to-know list.

I nod. "Right, and the guy who took over the gang when Chico went down was none other than Reynaldo Valdez. They call him Renny; he is Luis's brother."

"Who were the victims in the double murder?"

"Two members of a rival gang who were disputing Chico's preeminence in the community. No one will mourn their loss, but it turns out that murder is illegal even when the victims are scumbags. But the key is that the murders took place a year and a half ago, at least. Luis went into hiding out of town for quite a while. We got a tip he was back and made our move."

"I suggest we focus on the current situation rather than take this seemingly endless trip down memory lane," Henderson says.

"This is the current situation," I point out. "They are going to want you to do something to get Valdez off."

"We are getting very close to the time we will have to bring in the police on an official basis," Henderson says. "Once we know of a crime, and blackmailing is a crime, then we are bound to report it."

"It's not a crime yet," I say. "They have not demanded

or even asked that you do anything, nor have they made any threats. They have been smart about it; their meaning is clear, but they haven't crossed any lines."

"I'll take your legal counsel under advisement," Henderson says, as dryly as anything can be said. "For the moment I agree that we do not bring in the police. Doing so would invite our enemies to release their bogus, compromising information."

I'm not sure I agree with that reasoning, but I don't want to point it out now. I concur with the decision not to bring in the police, regardless of the tortured logic that gets us there.

Henderson continues, "On the seemingly endless list of disturbing aspects to this situation, there is still another that I haven't mentioned."

"What's that?" Laurie asks.

"My trial schedule is only public for the next three weeks. The Valdez trial is at least six weeks away. Even his lawyer is not aware of the date, or the fact that I will be presiding."

"It wouldn't matter if you were planning to preside," I say. "You are the chief judge; you assign the cases. If you were going to cave to the blackmail, part of that would be assigning the case to yourself."

"And the fact that our opposition seems to know my schedule?"

"Somehow they are conducting a successful surveillance on you, and it's more than just Vickers following you around."

"But the sweep of my home turned up nothing."

I nod. "It's just one of the things we don't yet understand."

THE LUIS VALDEZ INVOLVEMENT SURPRISES ME.

The timing fits quite well; once the murders were committed and Valdez went on the run, the potential setup of Judge Henderson began. Choosing Henderson was smart since as the chief judge he decides who presides over the various cases. Therefore the blackmailers wouldn't have had to guess which judge would draw the case; they would be blackmailing the person who would make that call.

But the players don't seem to fit. The X Gang under Chico Simmons had a reputation for ruthlessness and viciousness. They got their name because Chico is said to have had an enemy tied to a chair, then painted an X on his forehead and put a bullet in the center of it, as the victim unsuccessfully pleaded for his life.

Nothing in their past, at least as far as my knowledge goes, speaks to strategy or subtlety. This operation took tremendous planning and patience, qualities for which Chico and his successor,

Renny Valdez, have never been known. If anything, the gang has been said to have gotten even more violent and impulsive under Renny's leadership.

Chico was still alive and in charge when Eva Staley went to Henderson's hotel room, and it seems possible, albeit unlikely, that he would do such a thing. But Chico opening an account in the Caymans and funding it monthly? That is hard for me to imagine.

On the other hand, the case that got Chico killed involved a major drug-smuggling operation of a new and extremely addictive and dangerous drug. That would have involved the gang in a much more sophisticated operation, with people whose smarts probably extended well beyond the street.

Maybe getting Henderson to do their bidding started out as something other than an effort to get Luis Valdez off. Maybe with what they had going on, the idea of having a chief judge in their pocket was particularly appealing, with his specific usage to be decided upon later. In their line of work the prospect of their eventually winding up before a judge was likely. But at this point there's no way to know for sure their motivation.

But the bottom line is that as unlikely as it might be that a street gang is behind this, the text message that Henderson got is what it is. They referred to the Valdez case, setting Henderson up, and I don't know why they might have done that if it wasn't real.

One thing that neither Laurie nor I have verbalized but I bet is in the back of her mind just as it is mine is the possibility that the information the blackmailers have might be at least partially true. While I doubt that Judge Henderson did anything unethical from the bench, I have nothing except my gut instincts on which to base that view. I can't be sure that Judge Henderson is invulnerable to this attack.

I also doubt that the Caymans account is something he set up or even knew about. That it was untouched speaks to that. But I do think that the Eva Staley encounter could have been more than he says.

Certainly she arrived at his hotel as part of the blackmail attempt; the photograph proves that. But possibly he sent for her and she did more than just kiss him in the hallway and then leave.

There's no way to know, and for our purposes, at least for now, it doesn't matter. We've been hired to find the blackmailers and end their operation. Whether the incriminating evidence is real or faked, in all or part, doesn't change our mission. Blackmail is just as illegal either way.

Among the many disconcerting things about this situation is how much the blackmailers know. They know Henderson's private cell number, and more significant, they know his upcoming calendar, which apparently is closely guarded.

They are pulling the strings and dictating the pace, and we are left to react, and so far ineffectually at that. I think we may have to start shaking things up.

That can begin with Kevin Vickers.

Our going after Vickers has no real downside. He has been tailing Henderson, probably since before we were hired, so he has no doubt seen and identified us. If we approach and talk to him, it will obviously let him know that we have been aware of his involvement, but that's okay. At the least it will inform his employers that they have serious opponents to deal with.

Unfortunately, the upside is probably going to be limited as well. It's unlikely that he will cave and reveal all, even when confronted with Marcus. Vickers is a tough guy, a survivor, and he won't fold up on command.

We also don't have much to threaten him with legally. He

hasn't committed any crimes in following the Judge; nor could we prove that he's been doing so. There have been no threats or harassment, and as an ex-cop he would know that no case could be made against him.

Laurie, Marcus, and I have a brief meeting to decide how we'll go about confronting Vickers. Once again we leave it that I will go with Marcus to do so. I think this is starting to grate on Laurie's nerves, being left out of actions like this, but she recognizes that simple intimidation is key here. Marcus, Simon, and I are the most likely to get that job done.

Laurie is as tough as nails when it comes to the job; that was her reputation on the force, and nothing has changed. But that doesn't mean Vickers will have that perception, and I think she understands that. The bottom line is that she can be effective, but for us it's a smaller hill to climb.

"You think we should tell the Judge we're doing this?" she asks.

I nod. "We should tell him, not ask him."

"I'll call him." We both recognize that Laurie is the most effective in dealing with our client; he gets on my nerves and there is always a danger that he is going to light my short fuse.

Marcus has been following Vickers and knows where he lives and the places he frequents. His surveillance of Henderson each day has ended when the Judge has gone home for the night, so we'll wait for that. We'll do it tomorrow night, since it's getting late today, and we want to make sure that Laurie has had time to alert the Judge.

I'm looking forward to going on the offensive.

ACCORDING TO MARCUS, VICKERS IS PREDICTABLE.

He follows Henderson home, waits there for three hours to make sure he doesn't go back out, then leaves. Henderson has been equally predictable in that once he gets home, that's it for the night.

Vickers lives in Glen Rock, but always goes to a Clifton bar/restaurant on the way home. Marcus assumes he has dinner there, but doesn't know for sure. He has not gone inside because there has been no reason to, and because he understands the danger that Vickers might recognize him as one of the people working for Henderson.

Once Vickers leaves the bar, he goes straight home. Marcus has yet to see him meeting with anyone, though that could be taking place inside the bar. I tend to doubt it; my guess is that he communicates with his bosses electronically.

Marcus gives me Vickers's address in Glen Rock, and we decide to meet there at 10:00 P.M. Marcus will get there earlier to confirm that Vickers has gotten home, but we'll meet and keep our cars about a block away, unable to be seen from Vickers's house.

Simon and I get there at the appointed time and I text Marcus that I've arrived. He texts back, "Not here." I assume he means Vickers, though I suppose he could be referring to himself. Marcus is only slightly more understandable with the written rather than spoken word.

I don't ask who he was referring to. Laurie has said that Marcus is 100 percent reliable, and I haven't seen anything to make me doubt that. So Simon and I sit and wait. At ten thirty, Marcus texts, "Nothing."

At eleven o'clock Marcus shows up at my car in person.

"Has Vickers gotten home?"

"Nunnh," he says, shaking his head. I'm going to take that as a no.

"Maybe he's shacking up with someone." It's probably been twenty years since I used the word *shacking;* I'm not even sure it exists as a word anymore.

Marcus shrugs in response, which could mean either he agrees or doesn't care.

"We can wait a while longer."

This draws another shrug. This conversation hasn't seemed to have quite developed a rhythm.

"Let's give it another hour. Okay?"

Marcus nods and heads back to his vantage point watching Vickers's house. Exactly one hour later he's back at the car, a head shake indicating that Vickers is still nowhere to be found.

"Okay, let's abort. There's no reason this has to be done

tonight; we can try again tomorrow. Or we can grab him when he leaves the Judge's house tomorrow."

This gets another nod from Marcus, and all of a sudden he is gone. I turn to Simon. "He's a chatty guy, isn't he?"

Simon just looks at me and doesn't say a word, or even bark. I think there's quite a bit of Marcus in Simon.

Once we're on the road back, I decide to call Laurie and tell her about the failed operation. Just as I'm about to do so, my cell phone rings and I see by the caller ID that it's her.

"I was just going to call you."

"What the hell happened?" She sounds stressed.

"Nothing. Absolutely nothing."

"What do you mean?"

"He never showed."

"So you never saw Vickers tonight? Is that what you're saying?"

"That's what I'm saying. Relax, Laurie. You sound stressed."

"That's because I'm stressed. Vickers is dead, Corey."

"Tell me what you know."

"It was just reported on television. His body was found in front of Kennedy High School. That's all they're saying. No cause of death, no mention of suspects."

"We need to get the details. I'll call Pete in the morning and pump him for information."

"I'm relieved. I was afraid you and Marcus were involved."

I'm surprised by the question. "You thought we might have murdered Vickers? You don't know your teammates better than that?"

"Not murdered. But it could have escalated, and he could have pulled a gun on you. It's happened before. Marcus can be dangerous in situations like that."

"Marcus has a tendency to kill people?"

"In self-defense, or to prevent a murder."

This conversation is annoying me. "Laurie, we never saw Vickers, so this wasn't us. When and if we decide to murder someone, you'll be the first one I tell."

VICKERS'S BODY WAS FOUND ON THE STEPS OF WHAT IS CALLED KENNEDY High School.

That used to be its real name. Now it is officially the John F. Kennedy Educational Complex, which means that the people naming it must have an Insecurity Complex. By all accounts the new name hasn't improved the teacher-student ratio, or the class size, or the academic proficiency ratings. But it sounds cool.

Vickers was shot once through the forehead, from a distance police are initially estimating at twenty feet. I doubt it is much consolation to him, but his killers were no slouches; they have almost certainly done this before.

His body was left propped up on the steps of the school at around ten o'clock last night. He apparently looked as though he was there to greet arriving students; obviously his killers had no desire to hide their handiwork.

A 911 call to the police, made from what must be the last pay phone on planet Earth, revealed the existence and location of the body. It could have been made by a neighborhood person who for some reason was on school property at that hour, most likely not to check out the library. Or it could even have been made by the killers themselves, anxious to get the word out.

Laurie has gotten this information in a conversation early this morning with Pete Stanton. It's nothing that won't soon be public anyway, so he was fine in sharing it. He also spent some time pressing her as to why she was so anxious to know about it, and she deflected that by saying we would be back to him soon.

This is why we're back in Judge Henderson's chambers. He called us when he heard about the murder, but we were going to call him anyway. It's time to make some decisions.

"This brings it to a new level," I say. "We are not just dealing with blackmailers, we are dealing with murderers."

"We already knew that," Henderson says. "Luis Valdez is not on trial for jaywalking or keeping a library book out past the return date."

"Fair point," I say, "but those were gang, street killings. Bad as that is, there is an obvious difference here. This is in furtherance of blackmail."

"So you believe it to be connected to our situation?"

"Of course."

Laurie says, "The high school is in the neighborhood that the X Gang considers its turf. The implications are obvious, as are our obligations."

"Meaning?"

"We have information directly related to a crime, in this case murder. We are required by law to report this." She adds pointedly, "You have the same obligation, Judge."

"What is our knowledge? All we know is that the late

Mr. Vickers was at some point following me." Henderson seems anxious, if not desperate, to keep this under wraps.

"It wasn't 'at some point,'" I say. "It was every day, including yesterday, the day he died. And it was shortly before we were going to question him, which is interesting in itself."

Henderson won't drop it. "And maybe he went to the bar afterwards and got into an argument over money, or baseball, or a woman. Maybe that's why he was killed. This man was not a priest."

"Maybe," Laurie says, "that is for the police to determine after they have all the facts."

"I do not want my involvement in any of this to be made public. You must exercise great care to see that does not happen."

Laurie nods. "I think that can be handled."

"Then handle it. You have assumed responsibility for it."

"I think Andy should be involved," Laurie says. "On a limited basis. You have legal rights that need to be protected."

Henderson looks like he's about to argue the point, but then seems to think better of it. Instead he nods. "Fair enough. Keep that basis limited."

Laurie and I leave. As soon as we're in the car, she says, "I'm worried; our client is not thinking clearly. I'm afraid he's going to do something counterproductive. Extremely counterproductive."

"He ultimately listened to us."

She nods. "This time. But he's scared and under a lot of stress; he's also used to being in total control. Not a good combination."

She places a call to Pete telling him that we need to see him right away, on an issue related to the Vickers murder. He knows that we would not be wasting his time, so he asks us to come right in.

She then calls Andy, fills him in on what's going on, and he agrees to meet us there. We'll have a brief meeting outside before going in, to make sure we're on the same page.

On the way we talk about how we are going to handle it. Once we do, she says, "Andy should play the lead role. We want to reveal as little as possible, and he is better equipped to know the legal boundaries."

I'm okay with that, but something else is bothering me. "You think it's a coincidence that Vickers got killed on the same night that we were going to talk to him?"

"I've never believed in coincidences, and there is nothing about this that causes me to start now."

"Agreed. Which means that his employers were afraid he might be willing to pass on information. But what troubles me is how they knew we were making our move last night."

"Maybe we are the ones that are being spied on electronically."

I nod. "Let's have that checked out."

THIS TIME ANDY IS ALREADY WAITING FOR US AT THE PRECINCT.

He hasn't gone in to see Pete yet, so he's amusing himself by trading insults with the desk sergeant. It is not that difficult to see why most cops can't stand him. They already naturally despise defense attorneys, and when they're as sarcastic and irritating as Andy, it's amazing they haven't shot him. Yet.

I'm finally starting to get used to referring to cops as *they,* instead of *we*. It's a slow process; I was a cop for a lot of years, and I was proud of it for every one of them.

We step outside for a few minutes to discuss how we are going to deal with the meeting. Andy catches on right away and promises to handle it in the way we have decided on.

We head back in and find Pete waiting for us. After exchanging very few pleasantries, he says, "Okay. Tell me about Vickers."

"First let's set the terms," Andy says.

Pete can barely stifle a moan. "Here we go. . . ."

"It's pretty simple. My colleagues are about to give you some information. Since it's part of an ongoing investigation that they are conducting, and since they are extraordinarily talented at what they do, it is likely they will be able to provide more information in the future. In return, should you happen to accidentally stumble upon anything worthwhile on your own, we expect the same courtesy."

"If you have information relating to a murder, you are obligated to turn it over," Pete says.

"Which is why we are here; we are nothing if not good citizens. So we're agreed?"

"It will depend on the circumstances."

"Pete, you might want to take the deal," Andy says. "The last time you solved a murder case on your own was during the Clinton administration."

"You're an asshole," Pete says, then turns to Laurie and me. "Let's hear what you've got."

As agreed, Andy nods and turns the floor over to me. "We were aware that Vickers had been following Judge Henderson every day . . . from the time he left home in the morning until he got home at night."

Pete doesn't bother concealing his surprise. "Why was he doing that?"

"We were going to find out last night, or at least try to. We waited at his house, but he never showed up. Turns out he had a good excuse; his body was in front of Kennedy High School."

"I meant why was he following the Judge?"

Andy intervenes. "Here's where it gets tricky. I'm going to go out on a limb and assume you understand the concept of attorney-client privilege. So there are some things we can say, and some not. There is a line we can't cross."

Pete nods his understanding, so Andy continues, "And what I am about to say is confidential; it is for you only."

Another nod from Pete. "I'll keep it that way if I can."

Andy doesn't argue the point; I'm sure he knows that some developments might come up that would force Pete to include others. After all, this is an investigation. "There are people, identities currently unknown, who are attempting to blackmail the Judge."

"Blackmail is a crime," Pete says.

Andy turns to Laurie and me. "Didn't I tell you he was smart as a whip?" Then Andy says to Pete, "They have never actually crossed a line and made any demands; based on what they've done so far, there would not be a prosecution. But they have made their intentions clearly but indirectly known."

"What did they want?"

"They claimed their demands, when forthcoming, would relate to an upcoming murder trial for one Luis Valdez."

Pete nods, understanding immediately. "The high school is in the X Gang's neighborhood. What were they trying to hold over the Judge?"

"You know that attorney-client privilege line that I told you we can't cross?" Andy asks. "You're attempting to cross it. Suffice it to say that the material they would use against the Judge was simultaneously planted and faked. It has no merit whatsoever."

"What is the Judge going to do?"

"The line? Remember the line I mentioned?" Andy responds. "Now, what do you know about the murder that we don't?"

"Not much; it's too early. I already told Laurie what we know. One new development: there was twenty-five thousand dollars in cash in Vickers's apartment."

"Anything like a client list? Any connection to Renny Valdez and the X Gang?"

"Not yet. But we'll start looking at it now. Who should I contact if there's anything else that comes up that I can share?"

"Laurie or me," I say. "And one of us will keep you updated on our progress, to the extent that we can."

"Meanwhile, I think we'll be talking to Renny Valdez," Pete says.

I nod. "I expect we will as well."

"You'll get as much out of him as we will. Zero."

"We'll get a sense of him," I say.

"I've already gotten a sense of him in the past. So I suggest you bring Marcus with you." Pete then points to Andy. "Leave him at home."

THERE IS NO WAY PETE CAN KEEP THE BLACKMAILING COMPLETELY SECRET.

I'm sure that everyone in the room knew that. He's part of a department, even though he is the captain of the Homicide Division. He has people below him that are going to be part of this investigation, and he has people above him who are going to want to know what is going on.

Pete will not be able to identify Renny Valdez and the X Gang as prime suspects without sharing why he's doing so. That's just not how department investigations work.

What Andy was driving for were two things. Number one, for Pete to keep the people with knowledge of the blackmail attempt down to a small number, on a need-to-know basis. Number two, and most important, to keep it from going public. That would represent a monumental failure, and the department would get the full blame, to say nothing of the wrath of Judge Henderson.

If you're a cop in charge of other cops, you do not want to piss off the chief judge in your jurisdiction.

Laurie is about to drop me off at my house when her cell phone rings. It's the Judge; he seems to prefer her for contacts between him and our team. That's fine with me and probably better for the overall situation.

Generally speaking, Laurie is much more tactful than I am and handles people better. Judge Henderson pisses me off to the point that I might just shoot him myself. Then, once word got out that we were shooting our clients, that might put a damper on our newly formed business. Once we're better established, client shooting wouldn't be that big a deal. But for now, Laurie is best dealing with the Judge.

All I can hear is Laurie's side of the conversation, which is not terribly enlightening. All she says, after hello, is "Yes," then "Tell me the details," then "Have you decided what you plan to do?" Finally she says, "I'll talk to Corey and get back to you."

She hangs up and immediately fulfills her vow to "talk to Corey." "The Judge got another message."

"This is picking up speed."

"Yes, it is, but they still haven't made the explicit threat. He's been instructed to let them know if he will cooperate with them moving forward."

"Did the message specifically say the words 'moving forward'?"

"I'm not sure, could be. The Judge didn't read it to me; he was paraphrasing. Why?"

"Just doesn't sound like a gang kind of phrase. But maybe I'm out of touch on current gang lingo. How is he supposed to deliver the message?"

"By text. All he has to do is reply."

"What's he going to do?"

"He's thinking about it. He's deciding between ignoring it and telling them to kiss his ass."

"Are we supposed to advise him?"

She nods. "Yes, though I've got a hunch that he's once again going to make up his own mind. He sounded annoyed, like he's had enough of this."

"My advice would be to ignore it."

"Why?" She seems surprised; maybe she was going to recommend the opposite.

"I think we're best off if the other side has some uncertainty; if they are not sure what is going on, where things stand, it might frustrate them. They'll be more prone to make a mistake."

She nods again. "Good point; I hadn't thought of that. And maybe less likely to release the negative information they have on the Judge."

"I doubt that's a serious danger, at least not in the moment. It doesn't get them any closer to their goal. It also opens up new avenues of investigation that could be used to get back at them. The authorities might be able to get more information from the Caymans than we can, and they can certainly put more pressure on Eva Staley."

"Another good point, but there is always that chance that once they find out with certainty that the Judge won't cooperate, they might release the information just to get revenge on him."

"Maybe, but that's not my bet. I think first they will up the ante. They very well might be holding back even more negative information, which they can use to increase the pressure. They've put a huge amount of time and money into this, and their goal is to get the Judge to cooperate. To blow it all off now at the first sign of resistance just to get some revenge seems unlikely."

"I'll tell him to ignore it. Maybe he'll listen, maybe he won't."

"That's all we can do."

AS WE EXPECTED, THE JUDGE DID NOT TAKE OUR ADVICE.

He told them that he was not cooperating, that they should leave him alone, and that he would make sure they were tracked down and arrested if they persisted. He didn't use the words "cease and desist," but I'm sure they got the message.

It's been two days since he sent the text, and we have pretty much been on hold, waiting to see the reaction to his message. So far there has been nothing.

I had counseled that the Judge ignore them, to leave them confused and unsettled. Now they are ignoring us, and we are the confused and unsettled ones.

My best guess is that they are ultimately not going to take no for an answer, because it would mean abandoning a goal that they have invested a great deal of time, effort, and money in. Certainly they must have expected that the Judge might refuse, so they must have a backup plan to get him to reconsider.

Just because we haven't yet seen it doesn't mean we aren't going to.

No matter what they do, our mission doesn't change. We want to find the people that are doing this and put them away. The only thing that can deter us is if our client calls us off, which is entirely possible. If they seem to have crawled back under their rocks, he might not want us to expose them and risk having the entire thing, faked evidence and all, go public.

We haven't entirely been on hold; Laurie and I found time to have an argument over tactics. She came to me with the idea to have Sam Willis access Vickers's cell phone records through the phone company computers. This would tell us who Vickers might have talked to, which might hopefully lead us to his bosses. A second benefit might be that by tracking the GPS data in the phone retroactively, we can tell where Vickers had been, or at least were his phone had been.

She recommended this knowing that entering those computers without permission is obviously illegal.

It's not the first time we've had this discussion, and not the first time I've lost. Her point remains that it is a victimless crime, or that at least the only potential victims are the blackmailers.

"It makes me uncomfortable," she admitted, and her face reflected that discomfort. "Actually goes against my instincts. But I trust us to not abuse the information. In this case the end justifies the means. Maybe it's because I'm married to a defense attorney, but I've rationalized it to myself."

"You're advocating an action on behalf of our client that you would never tell our client about. And if we were caught doing it, we could wind up on trial in our client's courtroom."

She nodded. "That's true. But I'm still advocating it."

I backed off, just like I did last time, but she knows my feelings on the subject. If anything might potentially break up our newly formed team, this issue might be it. Which would be a shame; I like my partners and I think we're good together.

Sam promised her that he would have the information reasonably quickly, and one positive of it is that it will give us something concrete to do. We can take all the phone contacts and investigate them, hoping that we'll stumble on Vickers's bosses. We can also retrace his steps, using the GPS.

So now I have the uncomfortable feeling of not wanting Sam to get the information, but being glad that we will have it. Maybe I'm not so pure of heart after all; maybe I just want to appear that way. Maybe I have no intention of winning these arguments, but I want to make a show of demonstrating where I stand.

Maybe I am overthinking this.

We've pretty much decided to pay Renny Valdez a visit. That will take some planning, which Marcus is doing. He'll tell us when he has all the details down and has formulated an approach, then we'll move.

I don't think we'll get anything tangible out of it; it's not like Renny is going to confess. And it is unlikely that he'll make a stupid mistake, like wear a Cayman Islands T-shirt. But I want to get a personal assessment of him, to try to understand if he is capable of such an elaborate plan.

This time Laurie is insisting on going along. I could try to argue the point, but I have no interest in doing so. Laurie was a tough cop and I'm happy to have her next to me in a fight.

Laurie along with Marcus and me makes a damn tough team.

So for the moment we are waiting on the blackmailers to act, waiting on Sam to dissect Vickers's phone records, and waiting on Marcus to plan our "meeting" with Renny Valdez. If there is a good night to be waiting, then this is it, because tonight I am taking Dani Kendall to the Eagles concert.

I haven't seen Dani since our dinner several days ago and

have only spoken to her briefly, because work on the Henderson case has occupied my time. She seems fine with that; she is not the type to complain that I am not paying attention to her. She's not dependent on me, or apparently anyone else.

It's one of the many things that I like about her, but I'm not worried; I'll be able to find flaws in her sooner or later.

We share a love of the Eagles, but this is the first time that either of us has seen them since Glenn Frey died. His son has replaced him in the band, and even though I haven't heard them yet, I think that was a great idea.

The concert is absolutely terrific; the Eagles have lost nothing off their fastball. Great seats, great music, great company. I find myself staring at Dani with some frequency while the Eagles are playing. The expression on her face is simultaneously intense and joyous; it's like she has completely let the music take over and she is lost in it. I enjoy the concert; but she experiences it on an entirely different level. It doesn't seem like a level that I have ever been on, and I'm sort of envious of it.

Afterward we go to one of the four million great Italian restaurants in New York City. We sit and eat and talk for three hours, everything from sports to politics to books to movies. She is amazed by my knowledge of movies, so I spend some time showing off.

It's a great night of music and pasta and conversation and ultimately lovemaking. I can't remember ever having a more enjoyable evening, and I don't use the word *ever* lightly.

Clearly I've got to end this before it's too late.

"THEY'VE GIVEN ME A SECOND CHANCE," HENDERSON SAYS, FROWNING. "Really big of them."

We've been summoned to his chambers during the courtroom lunch break so the Judge can update us on the latest text. He shows it to us, and it's short and sweet. All it says is "You have twenty-four hours to change your mind."

"It's a sign of weakness," I say. "It means they don't have anything else to use against you."

He gives me a look of pure disdain. "They have plenty already."

"What are you going to do?"

"There's nothing I can do. From the beginning I had three choices. One was to cave and do what they wanted; that was obviously never going to happen. Another was to refuse outright, which is what I did. A third was to ignore them, play for time, and hope you came up with something. I tried that for a while, and I think you will admit that nothing came of it."

Neither Laurie nor I disagree with him; the plain fact is that we have come up with a big fat zero so far.

He continues, "So now I'm twenty-four hours away from seeing how this gets resolved, and all I can do is wait."

"Let's assume the worst, from our point of view," Laurie says. "They give up their goal to coerce you and release this damaging information. You need to have a strategy, both internally and publicly, to respond."

"I will deal with it internally. I've already sought some counsel. That doesn't concern you. The public relations side of it is more difficult and more troubling. I will be watching the reputation I have spent my life building torn down in a matter of minutes."

I am struck by Henderson's attitude. Most of the combativeness is gone, replaced by a sadness and recognition of what he is facing. I feel sorry for him; he deserves better. "It is that reputation against some faked evidence," I say. "You can win that battle."

He shakes his head. "The stain would never go away. You know that as well as I do."

Nothing is left for us to say, at least for now. He gives us his direction as we leave. "Stand down until tomorrow. If nothing happens and they back off, then let it go. If they go public, then go at them with all you've got."

It seems like a good strategy, and there is no harm in waiting twenty-four hours. We've accomplished nothing so far, so another day of it won't change anything.

Laurie calls Marcus and tells him that we will either see Renny Valdez tomorrow night, or not at all. I can't hear his end of the conversation, but my guess is that he says, "Ynnh."

We head back to Andy's law office on Van Houten Street. It's above a fruit stand, not exactly what you would expect for a semifamous, wealthy, high-powered lawyer. We're not going to see Andy; he's not in anyway. Instead we're going to see Sam Willis, who has his accounting office in the same building.

I've never met an accountant turned genius hacker before, or at least I don't think I have. Sam is absolutely not what I was expecting. He doesn't want to sit behind a desk, staring at a computer.

He wants action.

"You know, I could do a lot more for you guys than just this stuff," he says. "Andy doesn't let me, but I can handle the street."

"Sam . . . ," Laurie gently admonishes; she has obviously heard this before.

"I'm serious, Laurie."

"You want to handle the street?" I ask.

"Right. Whatever you need. Stakeouts, protection, whatever. I even have a license to carry." He's now focused on me, thinking that my question shows that I'm open to the idea.

"Laurie's in charge of personnel," I say.

She nods. "And Marcus is already in charge of street handling. He's pretty good at it."

"Okay, but I'm here when you need me."

Laurie smiles. "Good, because now is when we need you. What did you find out from Vickers's phone records?"

Sam gives us a detailed report on every call that Vickers made or received, beginning two weeks before we first saw that he was following Judge Henderson.

Sam has also accessed the GPS records to show everywhere the phone was at every moment during the same period. While there is no guarantee that Vickers had the phone with him at all times, it's a pretty good bet.

"Sam, this is remarkable," I say, since it is. I may not like the way in which it was obtained, but there is no disputing its value.

"Thanks. It's easy if you know the right buttons to press."

Sam's work will provide us with a lot to follow up on, should our investigation continue.

We'll know tomorrow.

"THE SHIT HAS OFFICIALLY HIT THE FAN."

Those are Laurie's words of greeting to me when I answer the phone. The digital clock on my night table says it is five thirty in the morning. It seems like shit is hitting the fan earlier and earlier these days.

Two things immediately come to my half-awake mind. One, Laurie gets up really early, and two, this is important.

"What happened?"

"They went public."

"How do you know?"

"Turn on CNN."

"CNN?"

"Yes. Not only did they go public, but they went national."

"I'll call you back."

I turn on CNN and they're in a commercial. It gives me time

to quickly put in my contact lenses, which will enable me to focus clearly on the disaster that we are facing.

I get back just as they come back from commercial. I'd be able to see the huge banner across the bottom even if I weren't wearing the contacts. It blares, in large block letters, NJ JUDGE FACING BRIBERY, SEX SCANDAL.

They go over the allegations without too much detail, alluding to the bank account in the Caymans, for which they flash some illegible documents. Much worse, they show the hotel hallway photograph of Judge Henderson being kissed by Eva Staley.

They promise further details to be forthcoming as the investigation unfolds, then cut to a panel of three legal experts. Two of them all but call for the Judge to be hung, pontificating about the sanctity of the system and the need for total public trust in the administration of justice. They must not realize that the justice system they are praising includes innocent until proven guilty.

The third panelist, a former federal prosecutor turned defense attorney, Doug Burns, takes what I consider the proper approach. He mentions Henderson's outstanding reputation and points out that these are just accusations that have not yet been tested.

Nowhere in the piece is there any mention of what Judge Henderson did to earn the bribe money, nor is there any indication as to how CNN came upon the news.

One thing I find significant. The announcer says that the network has spent the last thirty-six hours confirming enough of the story to run with it. That means that it was provided to them even before Henderson was given his twenty-four-hour ultimatum. So assuming the announcer is telling the truth, that last ultimatum had been an empty gesture; even if Henderson somehow caved, it would have been too late.

The only explanation I can come up with is that the blackmailers must have been sure that Henderson would not change his mind. Faced with the certainty that their plan to get him under their control had not worked, they set out to badly damage him.

The question that doesn't get answered by this explanation is why they bothered to give him twenty-four hours to change his mind. Once they gave the information to CNN, he would never have any incentive to go along with their plot.

I cannot imagine what is going through Henderson's mind right now. I hope he's still sleeping; the longer he doesn't have to know about this the better. But I'm sure he is being deluged by calls, especially from the press, seeking a response.

The only positive to this, and I'm stretching here, is that it makes our job a bit easier. We can take the gloves off, not having to worry about the reaction of the other side. They have already done whatever damage they can do; they've unloaded their arsenal. We no longer have to factor in whether we might goad them into action. They have made their move.

The ball is in our court.

We have two things to go on, neither of them terribly promising. One is the apparent involvement of the X Gang. While they seem to me unlikely candidates to mount this type of operation, they were trying to get Henderson to get Luis Valdez off the hook. Vickers's murder, and the location of his body, would seem to implicate them as well.

The other investigative approach is to run down the contacts that Sam Willis got from Vickers's phone records. We are sure that the same people who hired him are the people who attempted to blackmail Henderson. If Vickers had phone contact with them, or even physical contact as recorded by the phone's GPS, then we can identify them that way.

If it is Renny Valdez and the X Gang who hired and killed Vickers, then this would be a solid piece of evidence for the police to use. Of course, if Pete Stanton is doing his job, then they are accessing the same records legally that Sam Willis got illegally.

So we'll spend the day working off of Sam's list, and unless Marcus has a reason to delay, we'll pay Renny a visit tonight. We no longer have much reason to consult with Judge Henderson. He's given us our marching orders, and the ironic thing is that his involvement in our part of the operation is essentially over. He's been attacked and certainly damaged, and since we can no longer prevent that from happening, it becomes our job to get him some justice and revenge.

He's got a lot to deal with internally, and the public reaction will be extremely difficult for him. We can only help him with it if we catch the bad guys and expose that the entire thing was a setup.

Time for us to do that.

IT'S GOING TO TAKE A WHILE TO TRACK DOWN VICKERS'S CONTACTS.

Laurie has gone through and prioritized them, so that we can follow up on the most promising ones first. Easily at the top of that list is Miles Sloane, who I am going to see right now.

Sloane is the founder and managing partner of Sloane Enterprises, which is evidence that he's not terribly original at coming up with company names. Sloane Enterprises is an investment brokerage based in Fort Lee, New Jersey, and based on their offices, they either do well or want to appear to do well.

They occupy the eighth floor of a modern office building, and one side appears to be mostly glass. It overlooks the Hudson River, giving them a perfect view of the Manhattan skyline.

It's an incongruity that people pay a fortune to live on the Manhattan side of the river, bragging about their river view, when all they have is a view of New Jersey. There will never be poems written or songs sung about the beauty of New Jersey.

The Jersey residents pay far less, but can enjoy the more spectacular scene, since they have the skyline of Manhattan.

It is sort of like going to an expensive oceanfront hotel and paying extra to get a room overlooking the parking lot.

Sloane is at the top of the list because he used to be a partner of one Drew Lockman. At the time the firm was called Lockman & Sloane, but my guess is that once Lockman was out of the picture, it took all of ten seconds to get his name off the door and to change the stationery.

Drew Lockman ran what was essentially a Ponzi scheme, burning through almost $4 million of his investors' money, while living a life of amazing luxury. When this separate fund within Lockman & Sloane sank, cordoning it off from the rest of the firm was relatively easy.

As Andy Carpenter reported when he went through Judge Henderson's trials and decisions, Lockman was acquitted in Henderson's courtroom. The prosecution, according to the jury, could not prove beyond a reasonable doubt that Lockman didn't lose the money through terrible investments. Lockman essentially prevailed by using incompetence as a defense.

Lockman's lawyers also contended that high living was necessary for Lockman's work; he had to appear successful to attract investors. The jury obviously bought it.

Andy said that he was surprised that Henderson so clearly took the defense's side in his charge to the jury. Andy felt that it could have swayed the jury and could have moved some jurors that might have been on the fence into the acquittal camp. Andy felt it was somewhat uncharacteristic of the Judge, but not unprecedented.

I have no idea or reason for connecting Sloane or Lockman to the Henderson case. For one thing, they seem light-years removed from Renny Valdez and the X Gang. For another, Henderson ruled in Lockman's favor. Whether they paid the Judge off or not, why would they be targeting him now?

So even though the records showed that Vickers had three phone calls with Sloane, or at least his company, the connection to what we are doing seems less than strong. But then again, that's what investigations are for.

I wasn't surprised that Sloane was willing to see me. I told him that I was conducting an investigation relating to his ex-partner, Lockman, and that I was hoping to resolve it privately. The inference was that if I went public with the matter, it could reflect badly on Sloane or his company. I suspect that it might have been difficult to dig out from under the first scandal; the last thing he would want was a resurrection of that bad publicity.

I'm kept waiting in the reception area for about twenty minutes. This could be due to Sloane's being legitimately busy, or it might be a way for him to gain a psychological upper hand. I couldn't care less which it is. I just do what I do and block out all that other stuff.

When I'm finally brought back to his office, he's all smiles. He's on the young side, maybe forty. I find that every year more and more people strike me as being on the young side. He tells me to sit anywhere I like, which allows me to choose between two couches and six chairs. I pick a chair facing his desk, so he stays behind the desk.

"So what's this about Drew?" he asks, referring to Lockman.

"You read about Judge Henderson this morning?"

He nods. "Did I ever. What a shit show."

"He presided over Lockman's case."

"Believe me, I know. That case, even though I personally had nothing to do with it, almost killed this company. Is Drew's trial in any way connected to the news this morning?"

"Could be, but I wanted to talk to you about Kevin Vickers."

Sloane looks surprised. "What does he have to do with this?"

"Did you know Mr. Vickers?"

"Sure. He worked for me."

I certainly expected to hear that. I knew Vickers called Sloane three times. It had to be work related; they definitely don't seem like the types to have traveled in the same social circles. "In what capacity?"

"He was a private detective; he actually initially worked for Drew back around the time of the trial, trying to come up with information he could use to defend himself. That's how I met him. Since then I've kept him on retainer to investigate things as they came up. I deal with a lot of people and a lot of money, and sometimes I need information. He also did some bodyguard work for me, but not very often."

"Do you have any idea who killed him?"

Sloane shakes his head. "No, I didn't even know it had happened. I called him to give him an assignment, and that's when I found out. Sounds like it was a gang thing? He seemed like a good guy."

"How did you pay him?" I want to know if Sloane was the source of the cash found in Vickers's house.

"You mean how much? I paid him a thousand a month to be available, and then extra depending on how much work he did. Some months I didn't need him at all."

"I meant physically. Did you write him a check? Pay him in cash?"

Sloane smiles. "Cash? Does cash still exist? I think we wired the money into his account; I'd have to check with my people to be sure."

"Are you still in touch with Lockman? Do you still work together?"

"We don't work together, that's for sure. Drew is not exactly sought after in the investment world anymore. But he's still a friend and always will be. And he still owns a minority piece of this company, although I'm in control and he has nothing to do with operations."

"Even after what happened, he's still attached to the company?"

Sloane simultaneously nods and frowns. "He was acquitted, so we had no way to force him out. But we worked out a deal satisfactory to both sides. He still controls only his fund, the one he drained of money. It's walled off from the rest of the company; I have no access to it and he has no access to everything else. And his name was taken off the company, so our investors have no reason to be freaked out about it. It works out."

"So Lockman's fund is active? He has clients?"

Sloane laughs. "I would doubt that. Who would give him money to invest?"

"Where does he live?"

"I'm not sure he'd want me to say, so I won't. But it's not around here."

"So who can I talk with to find out more about the case?"

Sloane thinks for a few moments. "I guess Arthur McKnight. He knows all about it; he followed it more carefully than I did."

"Who is he?"

Sloane smiles. "You're not that familiar with the world of high finance, are you?"

I return the smile. "What tipped you off?"

"Arthur is a very serious player. He sold his tech start-up and just invests now; with my help his money has been very good at earning money."

"Sounds rich."

"His money starts with a *b* and ends with an *s*."

"And he was involved with Lockman?"

Sloane nods. "Oh, yes. Drew lost his money for him; Arthur does not like that."

"If I wanted to talk with McKnight, could you set it up?"

Sloane shrugs. "I could try. He might we willing, as long as I told him it could mean trouble for Drew."

I move the conversation back to the main subject. "Do you have any reason to think Drew Lockman might have anything against Judge Henderson?"

Sloane shakes his head. "No, that case worked out better than Drew or anyone else thought it would. That judge, and that jury, saved him from going away for a long time."

"Would you tell Lockman that I want to talk to him?" I hand Sloane my card. Laurie had K TEAM cards made up; they're not bad looking. They even have an outline drawing of Simon, which I think is a nice touch.

Sloane grins. "If I speak to him, I'll tell him, but I wouldn't expect a call, you know? He's spent the last year trying to put this behind him."

"The way to put it behind him is to be transparent."

"You sound like a cop."

"Been there, done that."

JUDGE HENDERSON GATHERED HIS BRAIN TRUST, THE SAME SMALL GROUP as before, for another crisis meeting.

Henderson did not consider a lot of people in the world close enough to provide guidance that would be both truthful and confidential, who would also have knowledge of the terrain he was about to navigate.

So once again only two people besides Henderson convened, at his house at 11:00 A.M. He himself had learned only five hours ago that the damaging information had been released, but this situation was urgent.

The two included Judge Robert Pletka, Henderson's protégé and second-in-command in the Passaic County judicial system. Judge Pletka was also Henderson's closest friend within the system, and thus his closest friend overall. Henderson's entire life was centered on his work and that judicial system.

Also there was Peter Tuckman, the head of public relations

for the Passaic County court system. Both Tuckman and Pletka had been kept apprised by Judge Henderson of everything that had been happening.

Henderson began by laying out the situation. The other men had obviously read and heard the media reports, but they didn't know all of the specifics of the evidence that CNN had received. Henderson didn't include a protestation of innocence because it wasn't necessary. Pletka and Tuckman had no doubt that Henderson had done nothing wrong.

After he described the situation, he said, "I've been informed that the Office of Judicial Ethics in Trenton has initiated an investigation."

Pletka nodded. "That's to be expected. They would have no choice in a situation like this."

"Right. So the question is, What do I do?"

They turned to Tuckman, who nodded. "I can give you my opinion on this, but first let me say that whatever it is you do should be done quickly and correctly. I say that because you need to get your position out there before public opinion has a chance to set. People essentially believe what they hear if not refuted, and if it is not refuted very early on, then those beliefs set in concrete.

"When I say it must be done correctly, I mean that you get one good bite of the apple. They're going to take what you say and try to dissect it and find holes in it, and they better not be able to. Because if you are forced to go back on your original statement, they'll pick you apart and you will lose credibility.

"So get your position out there right away, this afternoon, and make sure you can stand behind it."

Henderson frowned; he was not used to dealing with the public, or answering to anyone, and he was irritated at having to start now. He preferred operating in his private fiefdom, better known as a public courtroom. "What do you suggest I say?"

"That the charges are totally baseless and that you are calling for a full and complete investigation. You should pledge your total willingness to cooperate, and you promise to talk with any investigative body that may look into this. That you are outraged and look forward eagerly until that time that you can clear your name. Until then, because of the pending legal issues, you will have no further comment on the matter."

Judge Pletka said, "It sounds boilerplate to me; I've heard it a million times."

Tuckman nodded. "That's because it's the correct approach."

"Fine," Henderson said, "please draft a statement, so that I can release it."

"It shouldn't be a written statement. You should say it yourself, on camera."

Henderson shook his head. "No, I know what you're saying and why you're saying it, but I don't want to do that. It would feel like I'm giving the blackmailers too much credit and getting down in the dirt with the bastards. Please draft the statement."

As Tuckman started to do that on a laptop he'd brought to the meeting, Henderson moved the conversation to what his professional reaction should be. "I've got four choices, as I see it. I can suspend myself, pending a resolution. Or I can remain on the job but recuse myself from the Valdez case. Or I can remain on the job and recuse myself from all my upcoming cases, again pending resolution. Or I can just go on, business as usual."

"What's your inclination?" Pletka asked.

"Business as usual," Henderson said without hesitation. "It feels like anything else lends credence to the other side."

"I agree with that," said Tuckman. "You've earned trust and

respect, and anyone who doesn't want to give it to you can kiss your ass."

Pletka seemed unconvinced. "I'm not sure I agree. You'll get hit with the 'appearance of impropriety' argument. I would probably recuse from everything for a while if I were you, and definitely from Valdez."

"At this point the public does not know about Valdez being involved in this," Henderson pointed out.

"They will," said Tuckman. "Nothing stays secret in this world anymore."

Pletka nodded. "Right. Which means you can turn the tables by using the 'appearance of impropriety' argument against them. The charges are a load of crap, but you want to do everything you can to preserve the public's faith in the system."

"So I should recuse and you'll handle the Valdez case?"

Pletka laughed. "Never mind; disregard everything I've said. I don't want any part of it."

Henderson offered a small smile. "Then it's settled. Business as usual."

TONIGHT IS RENNY VALDEZ NIGHT.

Marcus has been working on setting up the best time and place to do it. We haven't exactly called ahead and made an appointment with Renny's admin; the element of surprise is going to be important. I'm not necessarily expecting any serious trouble, but it's certainly possible.

Either way, we'll be prepared.

It's going to be the whole team, minus Simon. Marcus and I tried again to talk Laurie out of coming, not because she's ill-equipped for the job, but because it seems like overkill. Besides, two seems more mobile than three, and easier to conceal until we make our move.

Laurie said that she would be fine if we were only two, but she insisted on being one of the two. Since I wasn't willing to back off, and since Marcus is the key player in this kind of operation, we're going to be three.

Renny travels in a pack, always surrounded by three or four of his people. Marcus says they are the same people every night, and they follow the same routine. Renny and his group spend their evenings at a local restaurant bar, which Marcus says is gang owned.

When they leave, usually around 11:00 P.M., the group walks to Renny's house, just a few blocks away. Sometimes they stay there, and sometimes they leave Renny alone, depending on whether Renny has a woman waiting for him. If one is waiting for him tonight, she is going to be waiting a while.

All of this is on gang turf, so I'm sure they must feel safe. That will change tonight.

Laurie drives and we head to the meeting point well in advance of the time they should be coming. We drop Marcus off near the bar, so that he can confirm that they are there again tonight. He will also see when they are about to leave and will go ahead of them and take his position near where we are.

At ten of eleven Laurie's cell phone vibrates and she looks at the caller ID. It's from Marcus, so she answers. All she says is "Are we good?" She listens for a few moments, hangs up, turns to me, and says, "Showtime." If she's nervous, she's hiding it well.

I get out of the car while Laurie remains, hunched down in the driver's seat. I assume my designated position tucked in behind porch steps. I haven't seen Marcus arrive, but I've learned that I never see Marcus arrive. Yet he always does.

I'm completely encased in darkness, waiting, and finally I hear people approaching. When they've almost reached me, I step out in front of them, and Marcus comes up from behind. It is perfectly choreographed; you would think we've done this before.

One guy is in front of Renny and two are behind, just as Marcus had predicted. The guy in front is my responsibility, so I hit him in the stomach, and when his head moves down in reaction, I club him across the jaw with my elbow. I hope he is a gang member and not a college student walking home after spending a night at the library cramming for an exam.

Either way, the elbow lands squarely and he goes down and out. The way I hit him, King Kong would have gone down and out.

Marcus's assignment is the two guys in the back, and two on one is a mismatch. Within moments, the only one left standing, the only still-conscious person in the group of four, is Renny.

"Don't move," Laurie says, holding a gun on Renny.

He doesn't move, but he does speak. "You are the walking dead. All of you."

"Thanks for sharing that," Laurie says. "Now get in the car."

Renny doesn't seem inclined to move, so Marcus grabs his neck from behind and moves him forward. I think Marcus may actually have lifted him off the ground, but I'm not sure. I open the back door and Marcus pushes him inside, then follows him in. I get in the front passenger seat, Laurie takes the driver's seat, and we're off.

I can now officially add kidnapping to my illegal-hacking résumé. I'm growing in this new job.

No one says a word in the car as we drive out of the area. Marcus has frisked Renny and taken away a handgun and a knife. He sits on Renny's right and has his left arm extended to the side, pinning Renny to the seat. It is like a seat belt on steroids, or like those harnesses they have on high-speed, insane roller coasters.

We drive to Eastside Park and go down to the lower level where the ball fields are. It's dark and desolate at this hour, so no one will see or hear us. We park just below the hill that they call Dead Man's Curve. It's a wild overstatement; it's not a terribly steep, winding hill. Giving it that name is an insult to real Dead Man's Curves everywhere.

I turn to Renny. "Renny, thanks for coming. Let's talk about Judge Henderson."

He starts to respond but seems unable to; Marcus's arm has crept up near Renny's throat. I look at Marcus, and he pulls the arm away. Renny is not going anywhere.

"I know you. You're a cop; the one with that dog." Renny had been there when we took down his brother, Luis.

"We're talking about Judge Henderson, Renny. Don't make this harder than it is."

"Who is that?"

"You know damn well who he is."

"Oh, wait a minute. That's the guy that took a bribe?"

"What do you know about it?"

"Just what I saw on television. He hung out with some hooker in New York, or something."

"You know her?"

Renny laughs. "No, I only hang out with nice girls." To Laurie, "You look like a nice girl."

Marcus's arm comes back up and presses against Renny's throat until he starts to choke. Marcus is obviously protective of Laurie, although she needs protection less than pretty much every other woman I've ever met.

"It's okay, Marcus," she says, and he relaxes his arm.

It takes a few minutes for Renny to get his throat cleared. When he finally speaks, most of the toughness and bravado are gone. "I don't know the damn judge, okay?"

"Why did you kill Vickers?" Laurie asks.

"Who the hell is that? Hey, you got the wrong guy; I don't know any of these assholes. Now let me out of here. You guys are already in deep shit for this."

I look at Laurie and she nods. Marcus opens the door and gets out.

"You just leaving me here?" Renny asks. "Where the hell are we?"

"Don't you have an Uber account, Renny?"

"I can handle it. And maybe I'll run into you and your dog someday."

"Renny, if he so much as gets a sore paw, you'll spend the last twenty-four hours of your life begging to die."

IT WAS THE FIRST TIME THEY HAD EVER BEEN TOGETHER AS A GROUP.

None of them had even known the others existed. They each were vaguely aware that colleagues would be sharing in the incredible prize, but no one knew who, and no one knew how many. Now they had the answer; there would be eight of them, plus the organizer.

Some of them knew each other and were surprised and pleased that the secrets had been kept. There were flashes of recognition because in many cases the reputations were well-known, and there were smiles at the pleasure of the revelation that they were all in good company. It somehow reaffirmed and validated their decisions to participate.

The setting for the meeting was incongruous, considering the people involved. This simple rustic cabin in the woods in northern New Jersey had none of the amenities they were used to. They sat around not a polished conference table but two old bridge tables pushed together. But none of them complained; they were not there on a luxury vacation. This was business . . . lucrative business.

They all had some things in common. For one thing, they were all wealthy, a necessary requirement to get into this "club." Just as important, the wealth they had was not enough, not for any of them. As the organizer said, only half-jokingly, "The problem with money is that you can never have all of it."

They were also all relatively young; the oldest of them was soon to turn forty-two. That was also mandatory; this enterprise would go on for a long time, and the fewer people who knew about it the better.

The organizer had not determined if there would be lines of succession, though he told each of them that there would be no passing of the baton. He planned to make that decision later; for now there was much more to plan and worry about.

Recruitment for this group had started almost two years ago, and the most recent addition was on board for a year and a half. Great care and energy had gone into the selections; one misstep could bring the entire process to a grinding, disastrous halt. So as best the organizer could determine, these were all careful, prudent people without skeletons of significance in their respective closets.

That they were all men was not necessarily by design. The organizer had made his choices based on diligent research, using his best judgment. That no women made the final cut was not planned, though it might have reflected a bias that he had about male-versus-female attitudes and morals. Women, he believed down deep, could not always be trusted to do the wrong, in this case illegal, thing.

Everyone was anxious to get started, so they did not spend much time in small talk and instead got right to it. They were impatient and therefore not pleased when the organizer told them that the final piece was not yet in place.

He did not tell them the reason for the delay.

He did not tell them about Judge Henderson.

He did not tell them about the murders that had been committed, or about those to follow.

He did not tell them the penalty that would befall them if they slipped up in the slightest way or even came close to compromising the confidentiality of the enterprise.

They would do as they were told; the details did not concern them.

The organizer would take care of everything.

WE WENT INTO THE RENNY VALDEZ ENCOUNTER WITH NO EXPECTATIONS, and they were met.

Renny denied having anything to do with Henderson or Vickers; he claimed not to know anything about either of them. Whether he was involved or not, that is what he would have said, so there's no significant information there. Nor did we expect any.

But we went through the entire exercise to get a sense of him, to get a feeling about it. All three of us came away with the same impression; if he blackmailed Henderson and killed Vickers, he's a good actor.

Not that we came away from it completely empty-handed. We did persuade a violent and ruthless gang leader to want nothing more than to kill each of us.

When I get home, I take Simon for a walk. I can tell he's annoyed at all the time I've spent away from him today. He's not used to waiting for me to come home from work; for many years we worked together. I feel sorry for him, and I miss the interaction, so I resolve to do better.

The walk gives me time to think about Renny Valdez and the chance that he is involved in Henderson's case. I've been troubled about it from the start; gang leaders don't generally employ the strategy, spend the money, or show the patience that Henderson's tormentors have shown.

The Vickers situation is another case in point. I have no doubt that Renny would be willing to kill Vickers or anybody else if it suited his needs. But why hire him in the first place? Apparently all he was doing was following Henderson. Renny probably has thirty people under him that could do that. And Vickers was an ex-cop; had he really sunk so low as to take on Renny Valdez as a client?

But the unchallenged fact is that the kidnappers wanted Henderson to intervene in their favor in the upcoming Luis Valdez trial. If Renny was not involved, and that is an if that we could drive a truck through, then why were they looking to get Valdez off?

One possibility is that Luis had more going on than just his brother's gang. Maybe he was involved with some other illegal activity and his partners in *that* operation are coming after the Judge.

Weighing against that is my knowledge of Luis Valdez. He is not the sharpest tool in the criminal shed; it's hard to imagine bad guys with the smarts and resources of these bad guys needing Luis for anything. And Luis is not the type that you can picture somebody going to all that trouble for out of loyalty.

Meanwhile, the press spent all day being brutal to Judge Henderson. It turns out that he was not only widely disliked by the lawyers who practiced in front of him, but also by the press that covered those trials. He never concealed his disdain for them and always acted in ways that made their lives more difficult.

In his defense, he would accurately argue that he was preserving the sanctity of the trials, that coverage by the press could in many instances taint and prejudice jurors. He also felt that sometimes they simply got things wrong, and that the damage that could be done because of it was significant. If the press didn't exist in the legal world, Henderson seemed to be saying, that world would be a better place.

He has put out a statement vigorously proclaiming his innocence, no doubt saying all the right things. The problem, at least to my mind, is that it sounds like hundreds of statements I've heard before, mostly coming from accused people who turned out to be guilty.

I'm sure that this is only the beginning. Henderson won't want to do anything to look like he's tampering with or influencing the investigation, but that will no doubt take a long while to complete. Meanwhile, the media will roast him on a skewer; information will dribble out that he will be powerless to refute.

As if to prove the point I just made to myself, I turn on CNN when I get home and see that they are teasing an interview that they will be doing the next day, with Eva Staley. They describe her as the woman in the salacious photograph, and obviously a key witness in the case against the Judge.

I'm not crazy about Judge Henderson, but I don't think he has done anything wrong other than being obnoxious. I sure as hell feel sorry for the guy, and I hope we can help him.

We're pretty much all he's got.

NOTHING SURPRISED ELLIS MCCRAY, BUT THIS JOB WAS COMING CLOSE.

Not only had he done it all, but more important, there was nothing he would not do. That lack of conscience, coupled with an awesome ability to perform any task assigned, no matter how difficult or dangerous, was the reason he was so valuable to every employer he ever worked for. He thought of himself, quite accurately, as the ultimate fixer.

It would have been wrong to call Ellis a contract killer. He killed for money; there was no doubt about that. But he could do so much more than that, and he was smart, whip smart, and in his business that set him apart from everyone else.

Ellis had been at the top of his profession for a long while, yet had somehow managed to stay under the radar. And when you did the kind of work that Ellis did, plenty of radar was out there searching for any sign of you.

But with all his experience, Ellis had been surprised by this job from day one. The identity of his employer was unexpected. This was not the kind of guy, nor did he come from the kind of world, that often needed someone like Ellis. And if the person did, maybe it was for a one-shot deal, most likely a contract killing.

But this job was for the long term, and the second surprise was the money. Ellis was used to being well paid; it came with the territory and was commensurate with his talent. But this job paid the kind of money he had never before seen and never would again.

The surprises kept coming after he was hired. He was surprised when he was asked to arrange for the hooker to entrap the Judge. He was surprised when he was instructed to kill Maria Burks. He strangled her in her car in her garage, but he had no idea how she could have interacted with his employer's world.

He was less surprised when he was told to kill Vickers, only because Vickers was smart and dangerous. He may have known more than he was supposed to, and the employer might have considered that a threat. Ellis was also taken aback when he was told to place the body at the high school, and he still did not know the reason for that.

Ellis was even smarter and more dangerous than Vickers, so he was fully aware that the employer might someday want him eliminated as well. That was why Ellis had taken so much of his money up front; if the employer made a move against him, it would be the last move the employer ever made. But that would turn the money spigot to off.

But Ellis was nothing if not careful; that is how he had survived for so long. So he had set out to learn what he could about the operation, which included following the organizer to the recent meeting he had set up with what must have been his coconspirators.

They were all wealthy and ill-equipped to deal with the kind of violence Ellis could bring to bear. But he had no intention of fighting them; what he wanted was to learn what they were up to. And he came up with a way to do it, which he would soon be executing.

But until then, Ellis was content to work in the dark and do the jobs he was assigned, even if they surprised him. The latest move that had taken Ellis aback was the release of the material against the Judge. It broke the blackmailer's code; once you've shot your bullets, then your gun is empty. So you hold on to them for as long as you can.

That was one difference between Ellis and his employer.

Ellis's gun was never empty.

And he would soon provide some surprises of his own.

EVA STALEY IS THE MERYL STREEP OF HOOKERS.

I just finished watching her interview on CNN, and even though I think every word she said was a lie, I wanted to give her a standing ovation. She was that good.

She checked all the boxes. She admitted that she was at the time selling her body, claiming that she needed the money to help her sick mother. But she's turned her life around, she humbly said, and is planning to get her high school diploma next year.

She assured everyone that she doesn't see herself as a victim, that what she did was not only illegal, it was wrong. She even shed a tear or two and once had to stop and ask for a tissue, which the interviewer sympathetically provided.

In its substance, it was not much different from what she'd told us. A man, she doesn't know who, paid her a lot of money to go to New York and have sex with Judge Henderson at his hotel.

She gave the name of the hotel, and while she couldn't give the exact date, she offered a fairly narrow time frame.

The CNN anchor interjects that they have confirmed that Judge Henderson was at the hotel at a date that fits her story. The anchor also cajoles her into revealing how much she was paid, and she says three thousand dollars.

Hopefully it was enough to save her poor mother.

The anchor questions why the mysterious benefactor came up with the three grand, and she says that she doesn't know, but that he mentioned something about repaying a favor. She also claims that the Judge, whose name she didn't even know at the time, knew she was coming, and certainly knew why.

She also says that she hasn't seen the man who paid her, or Judge Henderson, since that night. But that's okay, according to Eva, because she wants nothing more to do with her past life. And did she mention that she's getting her high school diploma?

Anyone on the planet who watched this interview believes there is a chance that she is telling the truth. I admit that I fall into this category as well; I wasn't there that night. For all I know she and the Judge could have ordered chocolate-covered cherries and champagne through room service and gone at it all night.

But if she's telling the truth, the implications are substantial. She wouldn't tell the truth about the encounter but lie about how it was set up. So if the Judge was expecting and welcoming her to his room, then someone *did* pay her to do it. Someone who could conceivably have been repaying a legal favor the Judge had done. Or someone who was doing it to set the Judge up for a framing.

Bottom line is that I don't believe her, but I've been wrong before.

The entire day has been an unmitigated disaster for Judge Henderson; the tour-de-force, televised Eva Staley performance was merely the capper.

The Office of Judicial Ethics released a statement saying that they are aware of the charges raised in the media and are conducting an immediate and complete investigation. They caution that the Judge, like anyone else, is entitled to the presumption of innocence, and they mention his long record of service. They will have no further comments until the investigation is completed, but didn't provide an expected time frame for that.

Left out of the statement, but obviously leaked to the media afterward, is the news that all of Judge Henderson's cases in the relevant period will be examined and his decisions scrutinized. If the Judge did something improper for which he reaped benefits, they are going to find it.

The Judge, for his part, is described in the media as having circled the wagons, desperate for a way out of this mess. He's said nothing beyond the original statement he released, and that is not helping. Of course, responding to questions begins a never-ending process, which would ultimately be worse. Anything he might say would be parsed and analyzed for discrepancies and flaws, and ultimately some would be found even if he was attempting to be truthful and accurate.

This must be a completely humiliating experience for Judge Henderson; vindication in matters like this can never be complete. There will always be doubts.

Tonight I'm meeting Richard Wallace for a drink at a bar in Paramus. Richard is the lead prosecutor in Passaic County. I've known him for years; we worked together on a bunch of cases. He's a good guy and as straight a shooter as exists on the planet.

We chitchat for a while and he asks me how I'm handling retirement, since he is near that point himself. I tell him I'm not retired, which cuts that part of the conversation rather short. I also tell him that while I'm glad we could catch up, it's for my new job that I want to talk to him.

Richard is prosecuting the Luis Valdez case; he's been on it since the murders were committed, and now that Luis has been captured and charged, Richard is taking it to trial. "Tell me your impression of Valdez," I say.

"Why?"

"It has to do with a case I'm working on."

"This about Judge Henderson?"

"What makes you say that?"

"The word is out that someone was trying to fix the Valdez case and that's why they were blackmailing the Judge."

There truly are no secrets in this world. "I'm really not at liberty to say. Attorney-client . . . you know how that is."

"You're not an attorney. Are you guys working for Andy? Is Andy working for Henderson? Now that would be as high as irony gets. Henderson and Andy can't stand each other."

This is not moving along. "Can you tell me about Valdez?"

"Okay. He's a piece of garbage; he would put a bullet in your brain and it wouldn't ruin his dinner."

"Is he smart?"

Wallace laughs. "Smart? He should be watered twice a day."

"So Renny is the brains of the family?"

"Luis makes Renny look like Stephen Hawking."

"Was Luis working for anyone else besides his brother? Is there anyone with a lot of money and a lot of smarts who would be desperate to get Luis out?"

"Look, Corey, I didn't write my dissertation on Luis Valdez. I don't claim to know everything about him, and I sure as hell don't want to. But this guy is not running Mensa meetings in jail. And his brother is all he's got; without Renny, Luis would have starved to death a long time ago."

"So it's Renny or no one."

"I don't know what you're looking for, so I can't answer you one way or the other on the bottom line here, but I can tell you this: as far as wanting Luis out of jail, and having resources to try and make it happen, it is definitely Renny or no one."

ELLIS MCCRAY HAD EIGHT MEN TO CHOOSE FROM.

They had come from all across the country for the meeting with the organizer. Ellis did not know what the meeting was about, but he knew that the secret to the entire operation rested with these people.

Ellis doubted that any of the eight would cause him a problem, so he picked the two closest geographically. It would cut down on his travel.

They were Gerald Stidham and Donald Crossland, based in Boston and Philadelphia, respectively. Once they went back home, they were easy to trace. All Ellis had to do was google them; these were prominent people. He learned their places of work, then followed them home to learn where they lived.

Ellis had no intention of confronting either of them; that would create the danger that one of them would go to the organizer and report Ellis's actions. That would be a disaster, counterproductive to what Ellis was trying to accomplish. What he wanted was to learn what the hell was going on, how these people were going to profit from their elaborate scheme.

Once he did that, he could either turn the profit for himself or use it to pressure his employer for far more money than Ellis was making, as substantial as that was. His actions would depend on what he learned.

Ellis was extraordinarily talented; it was the reason that the organizer had found and hired him in the first place. One of the talents was technological, and included in that was the ability to place virtually undetectable wiretaps and listening devices.

It took two days in each city, but Ellis completed the installation of surveillance on both Stidham and Crossland. He could now listen in to everything they said, at home and on the phone. Sooner or later they would unknowingly reveal to him what was going on.

Once he had that knowledge, all bets would be off.

JUDGE HENRY HENDERSON WAS PRONOUNCED DEAD AT 8:15 A.M.

That he was dead was fairly easy to detect, since his body had been hanging from a beam in his house since the night before.

His housekeeper found him when she arrived; his neck was in a makeshift noose made with heavy outdoor electrical wire. She screamed and then vomited, perhaps simultaneously, as she ran out of the house. Not carrying a cell phone, she ran to a neighbor and managed to convey what had happened. The neighbor called 911.

The coroner and homicide cops descended on the scene, and their trained eyes immediately identified it as a suicide. An autopsy would be conducted, but the cause of death was not going to be found to be cancer. It would be quite the coincidence if disease had claimed his life while he was hanging from a beam.

Pete Stanton was on the scene as captain of the Homicide

Division, and his initial reaction was to concur that it was likely a suicide. There were no signs of forced entry and the TV was on and tuned to CNN.

Stanton knew the public humiliation the Judge was enduring and also knew about Eva Staley's CNN interview the night before. No exact time of death had been determined, and even when it was, it would be set into a window of time. Pete would not have been surprised if Henderson took his own life either during the Eva Staley interview or just after.

Even though no one working at the scene called them, the media soon found out about it and came out in strength. Pete forced them far back from the area, while the coroner and forensics people did their work. Pete did not plan to speak to the press; that would be done by people much further up the ladder.

As far as the department, the media, and the public were concerned, this was no ordinary suicide.

Ninety minutes after the housekeeper walked into the house, Judge Henry Henderson's body was loaded into a van and taken to the morgue. Thus a life that only days before had been considered exemplary came to a sad and stunning conclusion.

The national media had previously run the bribery story low-key, except for CNN, which broke it. Now the coverage kicked into a frenzy, and the suicide was the lead story everywhere.

All but a few cautious, reasonable commentators immediately assumed it was evidence of Judge Henderson's guilt that he killed himself because he was caught in the act. Some even went so far as to say that the Judge couldn't bear the idea that he might be sent to prison, where he would be confined with many of the people he had previously sent there.

The others pointed out that just dealing with the horrible publicity and the news that had already stained his reputation might have caused him to kill himself. They did not assume guilt;

they just allowed for the possibility that the trauma and humiliation alone might have been enough to convince him to end it all.

A few colleagues professed shock, and pretty much every lawyer that had ever practiced in his courtroom opined on the situation. Andy Carpenter was a notable exception; he refused to be interviewed.

One of the lawyers even mentioned as an amusing aside that Henderson was known by some as Hatchet. The lawyer attributed this to the sharp, cutting remarks that the Judge would make from the bench. Testicles were not included in the anecdote, probably out of respect to the departed.

The Judge's closest friend, Judge Pletka, gave a brief, emotional interview, expressing shock and sorrow at the events. He said that he was part of a small group of confidants who were with Henderson the evening of his death. He said they had been concerned that the Judge had seemed upset and depressed, but they never anticipated what would happen.

Pletka seemed to be taking some of the blame on himself for not being more understanding of the danger that Henderson might do what he did and wished desperately that he had done more to prevent it.

Politicians were generally being evasive and were not rushing to microphones or Twitter to make comments. They characteristically wanted to see which way the wind would ultimately blow, and that might take a while. When a person with a record of service like Judge Henderson dies, they would ordinarily rush to extol him.

In this case they were avoiding that, in case investigations subsequently showed that he was a crook. Their attitude was that it was best not to praise or criticize until they knew whether either would prove justified.

The cable news networks trotted out a collection of psychologists and psychiatrists to talk about Judge Henderson's mental condition. All said that it was not possible or ethical to render a diagnosis, since they had not examined him. They said this just before each of them rendered a diagnosis.

The New Jersey State Office of Judicial Ethics issued a statement saying that the investigations into Judge Henderson's conduct would continue, though they would not have the benefit of his testimony. Possible criminal charges against the Judge would clearly not be pursued regardless of what the investigations uncovered.

Even as a chief judge, Henderson had lived and worked in relative obscurity.

That had changed forever in death.

THE K TEAM JUST LOST ITS FIRST AND ONLY CLIENT.

We're meeting at Laurie's house to discuss the situation, and we will be going to a memorial service for Judge Henderson directly from here. I've brought Simon with me since he is a member of the team as well. He won't be going to the service; instead, he will stay at the house and play with Tara and Sebastian.

Andy asked to be a part of our meeting, probably since the case was done under his firm's umbrella. That's fine with me and I assume with Laurie and Marcus as well.

I speak first. "I think we're all stunned by what happened; I know I am. The Judge was depressed and upset—anyone in his situation would be. But I never considered the possibility that he would take his own life."

"If that's what happened," Laurie says.

"You think he could have been murdered?"

"I don't know: I guess we have to defer to Pete and the others on the scene. But I'll be interested in seeing the autopsy results."

"Okay, but either way, even though we no longer have a client, that doesn't mean we don't have a job. We were hired to find out who was threatening the Judge, and that's what I think we should do."

Laurie nods. "I completely agree. You could make an argument that even if Judge Henderson took his own life, it was the blackmailers who killed him. Whether he did something unethical or not back then, and whether or not their evidence was real or faked, they still committed a crime."

"Exactly."

Laurie continues, "No one else will have any huge interest in making them pay for what they've done. With the Judge gone, it will barely be on anyone's radar."

"Don't forget, they also sure as hell killed Vickers," I say.

Laurie nods; I think she's happy and surprised at where we're winding up. She might have thought it would be hard to convince me. "I'd bet anything on it. So we're agreed? Marcus, what do you think?"

Marcus nods. "Ynnhh." It's amazing how he can succinctly put what we're all thinking into nonwords.

"So it's settled?" I ask. "We keep at it until we put the sons of bitches away where they belong?"

Andy speaks for the first time. "And I'm your new client."

"What does that mean?" I ask.

"I'm replacing Hatchet. I'm hiring you to do this."

"Andy—" Laurie starts, but he interrupts her interruption.

"I mean this. I knew Hatchet better than anyone. I couldn't stand him; he was disagreeable and insufferable. But he was also smart and fair and dedicated. I want to know what happened, and I want to clear his name, if it deserves to be cleared, and I believe it does. If I didn't hire you to do it, I'd hire someone else."

"It's possible you're not the irritating lowlife I assumed you to be," I say.

"Stop . . . I promised myself I wouldn't cry," Andy says.

"Okay, so let me put it another way. We're trading one obnoxious client for another."

"Much better," he says.

We spend the better part of an hour planning our next investigative steps. Andy asks that we give him progress reports as we would have given them to the Judge, then steps out to take Simon, Tara, and Sebastian for a walk in Eastside Park. When he comes back, we all head to the service, which is at a funeral home in downtown Paterson.

The place is filled to overflowing; if people were leery of being associated with the now-disgraced Judge, they are not showing it today. Judge Henderson's only son has flown in from California and speaks of the Judge as a devoted father and great role model. He talks about the incredible love affair his father and mother had, and since she died three years ago, he knows they are together once more. I'm not sure how he knows that, but I don't interrupt to ask the question.

Then Judge Pletka speaks eloquently, telling anecdotes about his friend and mentor. Both speakers put a human face on a man not necessarily known for his humanity, showing us a side of the Judge that many had not been familiar with.

To my surprise, the mayor of Paterson also speaks movingly about Judge Henderson. If the mayor's worried about the political ramifications of being associated with someone who may turn out to have been a criminal, he's hiding that concern for the moment.

Everyone has come to bury the Judge, and to praise him.

Tomorrow we set about vindicating him.

OUR APPROACH WILL BE TO CONTINUE ON TWO INVESTIGATIVE TRACKS.

They can be summed up as then and now. The *then* refers to the time that the blackmailers were claiming Judge Henderson did something unethical, worthy of being blackmailed over. Whatever happened was apparently so significant that it caused them to start their conspiracy; they began putting money into that Caymans account, and they took the additional step of sending Eva Staley to the Judge's hotel room.

But just because they deemed it significant, that doesn't mean it was real. They may have decided that the Judge did something that could be claimed to have been done for the wrong reasons, even if that wasn't the case. There's just no way to know, and with the Judge now gone, legally it matters less than it did before.

The *now* relates to what the blackmailers were trying to coerce the Judge into doing. It would seem that their bringing up Luis Valdez's trial answers that question, but it has never sat well with any of us. It's difficult to picture Renny Valdez, or his predecessor as gang leader, Chico Simmons, setting up that Cayman Islands account. It's even less credible that they would fund it.

But we have no idea why the blackmailers mentioned Valdez if he wasn't their concern. They obviously wanted him out of jail, but the reasons are somewhat less obvious. And with Henderson no longer around, do they have a plan B to accomplish what they want?

I believe that the answer can possibly be found by following the money. The blackmailers had it and had no qualms about spending it. Which brings me back to Drew Lockman. He's the guy that was accused of misspending millions of his investors' money. I had spoken with Miles Sloane, his former partner in their brokerage firm, but did not come away with any reason to think Lockman was involved in this current situation. But since they are no longer partners, Sloane might not even know.

It is far and away the case of Henderson's, within the time frame we are looking at, that involved the most money. For some of Lockman's investors, like Arthur McKnight, the money that was in the Caymans account is a rounding error.

The problem—a big one—is that Lockman was acquitted. Henderson gave a charge to the jury that helped ensure that acquittal, and Andy thought it was a somewhat strange thing for him to do. But why would Lockman look for revenge against the Judge who gave him his freedom? And why would Lockman give a damn if Luis Valdez was convicted of murder? They live in two different worlds.

Lockman's investors, after losing money with him and watching Henderson let him walk free, possibly wanted to exact revenge on the Judge. But that is such a stretch that it is not seriously worth considering.

The other factor that makes me suspect Lockman is that he

knew the late Kevin Vickers, using him to gather information for Lockman's trial. Sloane said he'd employed Vickers on occasion over the years, and Vickers had called Sloane at his office a few times, as shown in the records Sam collected. The coincidence cannot be ignored.

So I'll keep looking at it in the hopes that I see something I haven't seen before. I've talked to Sloane and gotten nowhere, but I don't know where Lockman is. Sloane had said that he might raise with Lockman the idea of talking to me, but held out little hope that he would be agreeable. I, in turn, have little hope that Sloane will even make the effort to ask him, and since I haven't heard from Lockman, I have to assume it's never going to happen.

Which brings me to Arthur McKnight. He's the investor who Sloane described as a billionaire that was ripped off by Lockman, and who knows a great deal about the case and situation. At my request, Sloane asked McKnight if he would talk to me, and that's why I'm here at his office on Fifty-eighth Street off of Madison Avenue in Manhattan.

The only kink in the plan is that McKnight is not here. The receptionist says that she doesn't know where he is, just that he's most certainly out doing something important. It's annoying, but she says it with a smile, and my disappointment is cushioned by this being one of the few reception areas in America that has up-to-date magazines.

A half hour after the scheduled time for our meeting, the elevator door opens and a man strides into the room. He's younger than I expected, maybe late thirties, and clearly in good shape. If I had to guess, his important meeting was at the gym.

He takes one look at me and says, "Come on back." So I follow him to his office. The entire place seems to consist of just his office, a conference room, and a small office outside his with desks seating two people. They're probably his assistants, but I don't know and don't much care.

Once we're seated, he says, "So you want to talk about Drew Lockman?"

"I do."

"What's your position?"

"I don't have a position. I am positionless."

"Everybody has a position."

"Everybody but me. But if it's any consolation, I'm trying to learn enough to develop one. You think Lockman should have been convicted?"

He frowns. "That's for sure; I even offered to testify, but they didn't call me. So at the end of the day the son of a bitch walked out of there with a smile on his face."

"You think he stole your money?"

Anger flashes in his face as he recalls what happened. "I know he did."

"How much?"

"A million five. Didn't exactly send me to a soup kitchen, but that's not the point. The point is he ripped me off and got away with it. On the list of things I hate, getting ripped off ranks number one, two, and three. Getting waterboarded would be a distant fourth."

I ask McKnight if he knows where Lockman is now, and what he's doing. McKnight doesn't, but warns that Lockman will be sorry if they ever cross paths.

"Are you aware of any reason for Lockman to have antagonism towards the judge in his case? Judge Henderson?"

"Is that what this is about? The judge who killed himself? Why would Lockman be pissed at him? He let him walk."

There's nothing for me to get here, but I probe for a few more minutes. McKnight is thrilled to talk about his investment prowess. He uses Sloane's company to do some, but not nearly all, of his trading.

"But I make all the calls," he says. "Here's a piece of advice. You want to make money, do it yourself. Nobody gives a damn about your money as much as you do."

"I'll keep that in mind. Good to know."

I head home and take Simon for a long walk. It gives me time to think, but in this case thinking turns out to be completely unproductive. When I get home, I make myself some pasta with already-prepared meat sauce, watch a Mets game, and fall asleep on my recliner in the fifth inning with them down three runs.

My ringing cell phone wakes me up. I have no idea why, but cell phone rings sound louder at night. It jolts me awake but doesn't necessarily worry me, because a quick glance at my watch shows it to be only ten o'clock.

"Hello?"

"Corey Douglas?"

"That's me."

"This is Drew Lockman. I understand you want to talk to me."

"You understand correctly."

"So talk."

"I talk better in person. I smile a lot and make eye contact."

He is quiet for at least ten seconds, thinking about it. Then, "Sure. Why not?"

"YOUR EX-PARTNER TOLD ME YOU DIDN'T LIVE AROUND HERE."

Drew Lockman laughs, but with no humor in it. "Really? Sloane lied about something? That's a shocker."

We're sitting in the living room of Lockman's River Edge apartment, on the thirty-fourth floor. It's about a five-minute drive from Sloane's Fort Lee office, so his comment on Lockman's far-off whereabouts does seem to be a tad off.

"He also said you and he were still friends and that you keep in touch."

"He's a lying piece of shit."

"Sounds like you guys have conflicting definitions of friendship. By the way, if you didn't speak to him, how did you know that I wanted to talk to you?"

"I still have friends over there. I founded that company; Sloane was just along for the ride. If it wasn't for me, he'd be bagging at Trader Joe's."

This is one bitter guy. "What exactly happened between you two?"

"He set me up. The whole thing; it was all his doing, and he laid it off on me."

"You're talking about the scheme that got you arrested?"

"It wasn't a scheme; that was all bullshit. I brought in all the money, and he blew it. But he cooked the books to make it look like me."

"According to the prosecution, you were off living the good life off the money."

I can see the anger in his face; I've obviously hit a nerve. "You believe what the prosecution said? If they were right about everything, how come you're not talking to me behind a glass partition in prison?"

It's a good question, and one I need the answer to. But I'll get to it. "You were partners and friends, you knew each other for years . . . why would he suddenly want to set you up?"

"He wanted me out of the company. The truth is, I don't think he cared if I went to jail or not. He wanted the show trial; he thought that would be all he needed to get me out."

"I don't understand."

"You read the trial transcript?"

I nod. "I did."

"After what you read, would you invest money with me?"

"I don't have money to invest."

"If you did, would you trust me with it?"

"There are others I would trust more."

He nods; his point made. "Exactly. So I made the best deal that I could. I still have my fund within the company; even though it's just sitting there empty. And I still have voting shares, just not enough of them."

"Why did he want you out?"

"That's the million-dollar question. The many-million-dollars question."

"I spoke to Arthur McKnight about you."

Lockman laughs again. "Poor Arthur. He's probably got two billion dollars, and he lost a million five in the deal. He should have a charity benefit. Or maybe I'll start a GoFundMe page . . . 'send poor Arthur McKnight to camp.'"

"He thinks you're guilty."

Lockman nods. "He's getting that from Sloane. Sloane convinced him—and everyone—that I blew his money. Nothing bothers Arthur more than thinking that someone took advantage of him. If he dropped a million five on the ground, he wouldn't bend over to pick it up. If he thought someone swindled him out of a nickel, he'd hire a hit man."

"What about Kevin Vickers?"

"What about him?"

"He's dead."

"So I've read. I know nothing about it. Kevin did some work for me during the trial, and then he realized where the money was, so he moved over to Sloane. It is what it is."

"You're bitter."

"You're damned right. But I'll make it back, and then they can all kiss my ass."

"What do you know about Judge Henry Henderson?"

"He's as dead as Vickers, or so I read." Then Lockman pauses. "No, disregard that comment; I'm just pissed off at the world. I didn't know Henderson, other than watching him during the trial. He seemed like a tough, fair guy, and he saw through the prosecution's bullshit. I was really sorry to see what happened to him. I thought about suicide at one point too, and I know that to do it you've really got to be in a lot of pain. Unbearable pain."

"You've had no contact with him since the trial?"

"No. Why? What's your interest in all this?"

"Just gathering information. Do you know anyone I could talk to about Vickers?"

"I knew his girlfriend; her name is Denise Tennison. I ran into her at a mall a couple of months ago; she remembered me and was friendly. I could give her a call."

"That would be great; thank you. Do you know Luis Valdez?"

He thinks, trying to place the name. "No. I don't think so."

I decide to try a direct approach, just to see a reaction. "There is a possibility that someone paid off Judge Henderson to handle your trial in the way that he did."

I see the confusion in Lockman's face; if he's acting, he's good at it. "That's ridiculous."

"Why?"

"Who would have done it? I sure didn't; I didn't even know the guy. And no one else would have done it because by then everyone I knew with money wouldn't even take my calls."

He thinks some more and finally says, "It doesn't make sense."

I have to admit that he's right about that.

THE WIRETAPS IN PHILADELPHIA AND BOSTON HAD QUICKLY TOLD ELLIS ALL he needed to know.

Stidham and Crossland, the two men Ellis had chosen to surveil, had revealed in their private conversations why they were a part of the meeting in New Jersey and more important, what the operation was about.

In a remarkable example of their naïveté, they had actually had a conversation with each other, reflecting on the meeting and discussing their plans to profit off the operation. They should have known that in this day and age nothing is confidential and one should assume that everything he says and does can be seen and heard.

While they weren't explicit in discussing the conspiracy, not out of caution but rather because they each knew that the other was familiar with it, only an idiot could have heard the conversation and not pieced together the underlying message.

Ellis was not an idiot.

He faced a dilemma. He was making big money, at least by his standards, for taking orders and working to advance the conspiracy. But by the standards of his employers, they were paying him peanuts.

Not only were his employers displaying incredible greed merely by participating in the conspiracy, they had also revealed a lack of conscience and respect for human life. Ellis knew that better than anyone else since he had been the one to commit the murders that they ordered.

Of course, Ellis shared their lack of conscience and respect for human life; that wasn't what concerned him. He was smart enough to realize that the next human life they didn't respect might be his. While they didn't know that he now knew their secret, they certainly knew that he knew enough to implicate them in terrible crimes.

They had the resources to hire enough muscle that even Ellis could not stand up to them. Once the operation was up and going, Ellis reasoned, they could decide to eliminate him like he had eliminated others at their direction.

So he came up with a plan that would make it impossible to eliminate him; they simply would not be able to proceed without him.

And he would get very rich in the process.

SOMEONE NEEDS TO STOP ME FROM SAYING WHAT I AM ABOUT TO SAY.

It's almost midnight and I'm pretty tired, but I can't hide behind that as an excuse. If the words forming in my head actually come out of my mouth, I will have no one to blame other than myself.

Dani is about to leave to go back to her house, and I don't want her to go. I want her to stay, but if I tell her that, she'll think I want her to stay, which I don't, even though I do.

Are we clear about this?

"How about if you stay over tonight?" I ask, making it officially too late to avoid saying what I just said.

She just about does a double take. "Excuse me?"

She's now given me a second chance not to say it, but I don't take advantage of it. "I was thinking it might be a good idea if you stayed over. Unless you don't agree, of course. Then I'll support whatever you decide. You know . . . to stay . . . or to go.

Whatever." The words are pouring out of my mouth in a stream of wimpy gibberish.

She smiles. "That's an eight-hour commitment; you sure you're emotionally ready for that? Maybe we should start in two-hour increments."

The truth is I'm not sure I'm ready, but I tell her that I am.

"Okay," she says. "We'll try it. But if you break into a sweat or start to get nauseous, just tell me."

Simon, who has been observing this from his own bed in the corner of my bedroom, barks twice. He's not expressing approval or disapproval of the conversation that he's just overheard, rather it's his way of telling me he wants to go outside for his last bathroom break before bed.

At this hour I usually just take him out in the backyard, but having just made love with Dani, it's going to take a crane or a shovel to get me out of bed.

"I'll do it," she says. "Come on, Simon. Daddy has used up all his energy, albeit in a good cause."

Simon doesn't need a leash, since the backyard is completely fenced in. He follows her out of the bedroom; they will walk through the house and go out the back door.

I don't know how long they are out there because I think I fall asleep. But the next thing I hear is Dani saying, "Corey, take a look at this."

Something about her tone makes me go alert; she sounds upset or nervous. I sit up and she walks over to me with a plastic bag. It's the kind of bag that she would use to pick up after Simon. Simon is with her, so at least I know that whatever is going on, he's okay.

She opens the bag and I look inside at what looks like a raw piece of meat, probably a steak. This is not computing for me, so I ask her what is going on.

"This was on the grass in the backyard; Simon found it and was about to eat it. I grabbed it because it seemed weird. Steaks don't usually grow in backyards. I assume you didn't put it there, so it must have been thrown over the fence."

"He definitely didn't get any of it?"

"I'm positive he didn't."

We keep Simon in the house and go back into the yard. I turn on the floodlights, so we can see anything else left out there. Sure enough, there is another steak, just like the first one.

"What's going on?" she asks.

"There is either a neighbor who gets a kick out of steak tossing, or someone is trying to hurt Simon."

"You think they might be poisoned?" she asks, horrified at the prospect.

"We'll know tomorrow. If they are, you saved his life." I am aware that in my exhausted state, had Dani gone home, I would have just let Simon out into the yard and waited for him to do his business. In this case that business would have included eating these steaks.

"I hope that's not the case," she says. "But if it is, do you have any idea who could have done it?"

"I know exactly who did it."

I probably spend two of the next eight hours sleeping; the rest of the time I alternate between shuddering at what might have happened to Simon, and planning what I am going to do to Renny Valdez.

Dani can't sleep either as she is shaken by what happened. We wind up talking on and off through most of the night. Simon doesn't seem terribly concerned by what may well have been a brush with death, and he sleeps soundly until morning.

At 8:00 A.M. I've kissed Dani good-bye and sent her on her way, and I'm in the police crime lab in downtown Paterson calling in another favor from an old colleague. Alan Mitchell has run the lab for the better part of ten years. We used to hang out a lot until he sailed off into commitment land and got married.

I tell him what happened and hand him the bag with the steaks. He knows Simon well and promises to analyze them immediately. It will take a couple of hours, so he promises to call me.

"Who would do something like this?"

"I don't know," I lie. I don't want to mention Renny Valdez, in case something winds up happening to him that I don't want to make public. And one thing is certain: if there is poison in those steaks, something is definitely going to happen to Renny Valdez.

WE'RE MEETING AT LAURIE'S HOUSE TO DISCUSS THE STATUS OF OUR INVESTIGATION.

I've brought Simon with me; until I find out what is going on, I'm reluctant to let him out of my sight. Besides, he seems to enjoy hanging out with Tara and Sebastian; it's nice that he's made new friends.

Andy is sitting in as well; that's the main reason we're holding the meeting here. Andy is now paying the freight and wants to be updated on progress, so he's an observer. He's promised not to interfere or micromanage and so far he's stuck to it. But he's a smart, experienced guy, so I think we'd all be willing to listen to anything he has to say.

I update the group on my meetings with Arthur McKnight and Drew Lockman. "It feels interesting to me," I say, when I'm finished. "These are big-money people, and the Lockman trial fits the time frame we are talking about. I don't know if Lockman deserved to be acquitted or not, but between him and Sloane, there's enough bad blood for something to have happened.

"Since Lockman got off, one possible theory is that Henderson was bribed by Sloane or someone else to have engineered a conviction, but didn't deliver. It would be a reason for the briber to want to extract revenge. But not only is that a long shot, it still doesn't take into account the Luis Valdez angle. If they have a connection to Luis, I have no knowledge of it."

"I think it's worth looking into Sloane's finances," Laurie says.

"What does 'looking into' mean?"

"I'm not sure," she says. "Any irregularities, some connection to Judge Henderson, or to other players in this case that we know about, or should know about."

"So you're talking about a Sam Willis fishing expedition?" I ask.

Andy interrupts, "I've caught some beauties that way."

"Yes, definitely a fishing expedition," Laurie says. "Starting out with publicly available information and expanding from there when we need to."

If I say I don't want Sam involved, then I'll get outvoted. When this is over, I'm going to have to decide whether I want to stay in this team. It's got a lot of good things going for it; Sam committing illegalities at our direction is not one of them.

"Okay." I wrap up this portion of the conversation by adding that I'm hoping to talk to Vickers's girlfriend, a conversation unlikely to yield any kind of breakthrough. Lockman had said he would try to set it up.

Laurie talks about the deep dive she has been doing into the slimeball that is Luis Valdez. She's been talking with cops who have dealt with the Valdez brothers and the X Gang over the years, as well as some former gang members that the cops steered her toward.

"It's not a pretty picture," she says. "Luis gives the word *lowlife* new meaning. There is no evidence anywhere that he is anything other than a moronic, violent, cruel piece of garbage, and that's giving him the benefit of the doubt. I also couldn't find any reason that he would be of value to anyone, other than maybe his brother. He's a loyal soldier to Renny."

We talk about our next steps, and Andy interjects some information that he has heard through the courthouse grapevine. "Every lawyer for every person convicted in Hatchet's courtroom in the last two years is coming out of the woodwork, looking for a new trial. Every ruling Hatchet has made is going under a microscope."

"Do they have a chance?" I ask.

"Walter Cummings certainly thinks so. I saw him at the courthouse today. But his petition for a new trial for his client was filed before this all happened. He's got other grounds."

"Any idea what they are?"

Andy shakes his head. "No, but maybe I'll keep an eye out for it."

Cummings's client is John Lowry, the IT guy who was convicted for killing someone in a bar fight with one punch. I met with Cummings about it, but he was typically reticent to give much information. There is certainly nothing about Lowry that would indicate he's involved in our case; the only reason he was interesting to me was that Cummings is such an expensive lawyer for a guy like Lowry to have.

The conversation is cut short when my cell phone rings, and caller ID shows it is Alan Mitchell. He comes right to the point. "The steaks were packed with arsenic. If Simon had eaten one, he wouldn't have lasted five minutes."

I thank him and hang up. I hadn't told the group about the events of the night before, so I now lay it out, including Mitchell's lab results.

Nobody says a word until at least twenty seconds after I finish.

Laurie speaks first. "Renny Valdez."

I nod. "He threatened Simon."

Andy says, "And if there are no repercussions, he'll try it again."

"There will be repercussions," I say. "Very serious repercussions."

"Whatever we do, we do as a team," Laurie says.

I shake my head. "No. Not this time. I will deal with Renny Valdez myself."

DREW LOCKMAN CAME THROUGH AS PROMISED.

He clearly believes that I am out to get his former partner, Miles Sloane, so will do whatever he can to help me along. That's why I am sitting in a diner in Teaneck at eight o'clock in the evening, waiting for Denise Tennison to arrive. She couldn't meet me until after work; she said she's a waitress at Applebee's and today is on the shift that gets out at 7:00 P.M.

A woman walks in and looks around, as if trying to find someone. She's attractive, but younger than I expected. Vickers probably had ten years on her.

I take a chance and wave. I think it's her, but if I'm wrong, incorrect waving is not a felony in New Jersey.

She nods and comes over to me. "Mr. Douglas?"

"That's me. I'm going to take a wild guess that you're Denise Tennison."

She smiles. "Good guess. You wanted to talk about Kevin?"

This is a woman who doesn't believe in small talk. I admire and appreciate that quality. "Yes, if you don't mind. I'm sorry for your loss."

"Thank you."

"How long did you know him?"

"October would be three years. We were talking about marriage."

"I'm interested in what you knew about his work, particularly in the months leading up to his death."

She thinks about it, searching her memory. "He really didn't talk about it much. But in the last weeks he was pretty intense about something, but in a good way. He thought he was going to make a lot of money. He said when it was over, we could go on a trip, to anywhere I wanted. I was thinking Paris." She smiles. "He was thinking Vegas."

"How was he going to earn the money? What was he doing?"

She shrugs. "Honestly, I don't know, but . . ."

She pauses, as if unsure of her memory, or whether to voice it. I prompt her. "Whatever you remember might help me find the person who killed him."

She nods; that's her goal in being here. "I sometimes heard him on the phone. One time he was talking to a man named Miles, at least I think that was his name. I don't know his last name."

The chance of it not being Miles Sloane is infinitesimal, especially since Vickers placed three recent calls to Sloane's office. "Miles Sloane?" I ask, just to confirm.

"I don't know. He didn't use a last name that I remember."

"Tell me whatever you can about the conversation. Please."

"Kevin was angry; it was one of the few times I saw him that way. He said something like, 'Miles, I'm a professional. I'm all over this guy.'"

He certainly could have been referring to his tailing Judge Henderson, which would make this a monster revelation. "Do you remember anything else he said?"

She shakes her head. "No. I'm sorry."

"Did he ever mention a judge? Or the name Henderson?"

"I don't think so. That doesn't mean he didn't; I just can't recall it."

I spend the next ten minutes trying to get her to dredge up some more recollections, but I can't do it. In the meantime, the server has come over and asked if we want to order. Denise doesn't; she clearly wants to get out of here. I order a hamburger and fries; no sense wasting a good diner.

I'm polishing off the last of the fries and just starting to ponder the potentially significant revelations by Denise Tennison, who left when my food came, when my cell phone rings. I can see by the caller ID that it's Laurie. "We have a bit of a situation here," she says.

"Tell me."

"Marcus just called. He's at the pavilion building on the lower level of Eastside Park. He wants you to come down there right away."

"Why?"

"He has Renny Valdez with him."

I don't even bother to wipe the ketchup off my face. "I'm on my way."

"I'll meet you there."

"No. Please don't."

THIS WILL BE THE SECOND TIME THAT I'VE MET WITH RENNY VALDEZ IN Eastside Park.

Last time was in Laurie's car, sitting with the lights out on Dead Man's Curve. This time the meeting place will apparently be the deserted pavilion building down below the curve. It sits on the huge, grassy expanse, in between the Little League fields and the full-size field.

Back in the day it contained a refreshment stand, but that was well back in the day. For a long time now, it's just been an empty building. According to Laurie, it's not empty tonight.

I arrive and park near the building. I shut the car lights off, which leaves me in the dark, literally and figuratively, although there is enough moonlight to get around. I don't know what to expect, or what Marcus has already done to Renny Valdez.

I can only assume that Marcus knew that I was planning to deal with Renny for his attempt to kill Simon. As a good teammate, he smoothed the way for me by eliminating the planning process. I have no idea how Marcus has gotten Renny here, but I have a feeling that a number of Renny's people are slowly regaining consciousness. I also imagine a lot of moaning is involved.

I don't even have to go inside. Marcus and Renny are standing in front of the open door, watching me walk up.

Renny doesn't look any the worse for wear; nor does Marcus. Marcus obviously thought his job was to get Renny here, not to soften him up. His instincts in this regard were perfect.

"You tried to poison my dog," I say.

"So?"

"So I'm just glad you're a stupid piece of shit who couldn't pull it off."

He doesn't answer, so I turn to Marcus. "I assume he's unarmed?"

Marcus nods.

I take out my handgun and hand it to Marcus. "Now we both are. Would you excuse us please, Marcus?"

He takes the gun and nods as if it's a reasonable request and happens every day. Then he just walks away into the darkness. His car is here so I doubt he's left entirely, but I don't see him.

"Just you and me now, Renny."

"Walk away, old man. You couldn't handle me on your best day."

Renny is a good fifteen years younger than me and seems to be in good shape. Certainly there is no fat on him. If he's afraid of me, it's not readily apparent.

I have three advantages. First of all, I am a tough guy. Not Marcus tough; Godzilla is not Marcus tough. But I have a long history of being in rough, physical confrontations, and so far I'm pretty much undefeated. I have my Marine Corps training to thank for that. Second, Renny tried to kill my best friend. Third, Renny tried to kill my best friend.

I'm motivated.

"I warned you the other night, but you didn't listen," I say. "You are about to learn that you should have listened."

He knows where this is going and decides not to wait for it to get there. This is not a guy who touches gloves before the fight. He rushes me and throws a roundhouse right hand, which I move away from just in time. It lands, but it's a glancing blow to the side of the head. No damage.

I learned a couple of things from the punch. One is that Renny is stronger and hits harder than I thought. Two is that he doesn't hit hard enough and is not nearly smart enough.

My assessment is that it's been a long time since Renny was in a street fight. As the leader of his gang, he hasn't likely been challenged much, if at all, and he is always surrounded by his people. So he has not been battle-tested, at least not lately, and he is going to pay the price for that.

I smile at the punch, though I don't know if he can see that in the dim light. The smile is more for my benefit than his; I am trying to control myself. I am raging with anger inside; it's a feeling I have had before and one that I hate. Not only can it make me do things I will later regret, but it will impact my ability to deal with Renny efficiently and effectively.

I have developed techniques to deal with this feeling, one of which is to change my outward reaction. If I appear calm, I become calm. At least that's the theory. Sometimes it works, though it's far from foolproof. Right now it doesn't seem to be working so well.

Now that Renny has taken a shot, it's my turn. He's still throwing punches, but I step inside them and throw a few of my own. They are short and straight, the hardest type to block and the ones that do the most damage.

I hit him with three or four straight lefts, and the old Muhammad Ali line comes to mind: "I'll hit you with so many lefts, you'll be begging for a right." Finally I throw the right, twice. On the second one I opt not to hit him with my fist, but instead I cross over and nail him with my elbow.

That puts him down.

He's bleeding and helpless, but conscious. I can see the fear in his face as I kneel down with my right knee pressing down on his upper chest. It has to hurt like hell, which is probably why he is moaning.

"You're going to die, Renny. Right here and right now. You don't deserve to live, and you're not going to. You're going to die alone on this cement floor, with no one to help you, whimpering like the piece of useless garbage that you are. You ready to die, Renny?"

In some strange way it doesn't feel like I'm the one talking; it's as if I am watching the scene. I hope Marcus is watching and I hope he intervenes, because otherwise I just don't know what is going to happen next.

It's hard for Renny to move and talk because of the way I have him pinned. He has no air because his chest is compressed. He seems to be shaking his head, and making some kind of noises, but if they are words, I can't make them out. I think he's crying, but in this light, I can't be sure.

I pull my hand back to throw the punches that will crush his skull and send his nose back into his brain. I know that when he is dead, no one will miss him, and the world will be a significantly better place. I also know that he has taken other lives, and his own death in this manner is real-world justice.

But suddenly I cannot cross that line.

"Renny, you have just had a near-death experience. Understand something. We can get to you whenever we want, and if we have to find you again, you won't be this lucky."

I push off with my knee as I get up, momentarily pressing his chest even harder. Then I stand and leave.

I need to find Marcus to get my gun back.

And to thank him.

IT WAS NOT A FUN TIME FOR JUDGE ROBERT PLETKA.

As the acknowledged second-in-command to Judge Henderson, the state Judicial Board has done the expected and named him acting chief judge. No one has any doubt that he will soon be given the position permanently; this is just a stopgap to keep things moving.

Courts in the county were closed for one day as a tribute to Henderson, as at least for the moment the doubts about his ethics were shelved. His actions are for the state to investigate and to determine whether he violated his oath. That process will most likely be slow, but has already been set in motion.

Part of the investigation is an analysis of his cases over the last two years. That is urgent, as just about every lawyer for every person convicted in Judge Henderson's courtroom is claiming that the client was a victim of a miscarriage of justice.

For now, Pletka's marching orders are to conduct business as normal, even though normal does not come close to describing recent events. The most pressing matter before him is to parcel out the various matters that were before Judge Henderson, as well as those coming up.

It will not be easy to manage. The department was already shorthanded, with one judge having recently retired without yet being replaced, and another having just undergone back surgery. Those cases that can be delayed will be, but there are not many of them. Every lawyer and every defendant considers their case to be the most urgent one on the docket.

Pletka gathered his judges for a lunch meeting to learn the status of the various cases, to analyze their urgency and potential for delay, and, most important, to assign Judge Henderson's cases. The other judges, while still stunned by the recent turn of events, nevertheless approached the situation with a "team first" attitude, all willing to step up and do whatever was necessary.

Pletka had discussed it with Peter Tuckman, and they both felt it was Pletka's obligation to do more than his share. It would be a way to show leadership and ward off any resentment that the others might be feeling for not having gotten the top job themselves.

So Pletka took four of Judge Henderson's upcoming matters, while not assigning more than two to any of the other judges. Included in the four was the key one, the one everyone would be watching, and that was the Luis Valdez murder trial.

Of the others, one was a simple breaking and entering that would likely be pled and not go to trial and another was a domestic violence matter. The third was actually next on the docket, the case of John Lowry, convicted of manslaughter in a bar fight. He was seeking a new trial based on an alleged judicial error by Judge Henderson.

Pletka told the others that he would handle that case because the prospect of judicial error by Henderson would be heavily scrutinized in light of recent events. Also, Lowry is represented by Walter Cummings, which means the defense will be vigorous and well funded.

For everyone in the room, it felt strange that Judge Henderson was not there to lead them. But the justice system was not about to grind to a halt, and they would do their part to make it run as smoothly and efficiently as possible.

Judge Pletka was their leader now.

COURTROOMS WERE NEAR THE TOP OF ANDY CARPENTER'S LEAST FAVORITE places list.

That is because he was only in them when he was working as a lawyer, and lawyering would have been at the very top of his least favorite pastime list.

It had never come close to entering his mind to voluntarily attend a court session when he was not working; he would have been just as likely to show up at a dance recital or poetry reading. He has often said this to anyone who would listen, and to some of us who have no desire to listen.

But today he made an exception, and that's apparently what he's called this meeting to tell us about. Laurie, Marcus, and I are waiting at his house for him to get back from court. We don't have to wait long, and he gets right down to business.

"So I sat in on a hearing today. Walter Cummings and the prosecution were presenting oral arguments in the case of *New*

Jersey vs. John Lowry. You remember what that's about, right? Lowry had been convicted eighteen months earlier of intentional manslaughter, after a one-punch bar fight that resulted in the death of the person on the receiving end of Lowry's fist."

Laurie and I both nod that we remember the case. The original trial was presided over by Judge Henderson and took place within the time frame of interest to us. I had also spoken to Cummings about it, a conversation that went absolutely nowhere.

Andy continues, "The reason I have been interested in this is because of Cummings. He doesn't do much criminal work, and if he lowers himself to do so, you can be sure he's getting a huge fee. Lowry is a tech guy, but he's a worker bee; he's not CEO of Google. With all the money being thrown around in the Henderson case, it just felt like it could be relevant."

"What was the hearing about?" Laurie asks.

"Cummings is seeking to overturn the guilty verdict and get a new trial. His first stop is this district court. He can then appeal, but it would be very time-consuming. He wants to get it done at this level."

"On what grounds?" I ask.

"That's where it gets interesting. One of the grounds is judicial error; he thinks Hatchet screwed up in his charge to the jury."

"Did he?"

Andy nods. "It's very possible. Here's the issue: For a defendant to be convicted of intentional manslaughter, he must have had a reasonable expectation that his actions would result in death. He actually must have expected that result. Hatchet did not tell the jury that in his charge; it can definitely be argued that he should have."

"So if you punch someone and it kills them, you're off the hook if you didn't expect that result?" I ask.

Andy nods. "Right. But we're talking about intentional manslaughter. The conviction could have been for reckless manslaughter, which is much less serious and almost always results in a much lesser sentence."

"What might the Judge say was his reason for giving the charge that way?" Laurie asks.

"Hard to know for sure, but there is an extenuating circumstance which could explain it. Lowry used to be a professional boxer and he's a huge guy. As a boxer it could be argued that he knew that his punch could cause death, that his fists were by definition deadly weapons. That came up during the trial."

"What's your view on it?" I ask.

"I think he made an error, though I doubt if the argument would by itself carry the day. But they may have more. Something that the prosecution said during the hearing makes this even more interesting, and it's why I called you here."

"What's that?" Laurie asks.

"The bar fight started when the victim mistreated his girlfriend in a way that caused Lowry to intervene. The girlfriend's name was Maria Burks, and she was a key witness against Lowry. She moved to Ohio, but about a month ago, she didn't show up for work one day and hasn't been seen since. It was apparently completely uncharacteristic of her. The prosecutors are trying to find out more about the circumstances surrounding her disappearance."

Laurie asks if Andy thinks that Lowry will get the new trial, and he says, "Very possibly, although Judge Pletka can be as tough as Hatchet. But the reason I think they might prevail is the fact that in addition to me and the participants, there was also the elephant in the room."

"The fact that all of Henderson's rulings are under a microscope," I say.

Andy nods. "Exactly. The courts are going to bend over backwards to give defendants that Hatchet convicted every consideration. That doesn't mean they will let Lowry off, but they might give him a new trial. The fact that judicial error is alleged here is key. And the fact that Cummings is the lawyer, even though they would never admit it, is going to be a factor. He can draw extra attention to what might ordinarily be a beneath-the-radar case."

"I don't see what it does for us," I say. "I can't picture Sloane involved with an ex-fighter who gets into bar brawls. Sloane is the type who wants to be seen with the rich and famous, or at least the rich . . . the Arthur McKnights of the world."

Laurie turns to Andy. "What's your gut?"

Andy thinks for a few moments. "Logically I agree with Corey, and it probably has nothing to do with your case. But there's something about it . . ."

He doesn't finish the sentence, but I know what he means. "I'll be very happy to be proven wrong. But one thing is for sure, it's as good as anything else we've got." Then, "I'm on it."

AN ECN IS A TYPE OF ATS THAT DEALS WITH THE NYSE.

If you don't know what that means, then join the club, because I don't either.

I'm sitting in the reception area of Equi-net. I've been sitting in a lot of reception areas lately; it seems to come with my new job description. When I was on the force, I did stuff; now I sit and talk about doing stuff, in the hope that I can learn enough to allow me to do stuff.

I've become something of an expert on reception-area magazines. They're usually old, which allows me to amuse myself by the sports, political, and financial predictions that the so-called experts have made that have already been proven completely wrong. One thing that annoys me is when the crossword and sudoku puzzles have already been completed . . . in pen.

Some people have no regard for those who would follow them.

In this case I haven't even bothered to check out the magazines because I'm spending the few minutes before my meeting reading the company brochures that are out here. I'm not sure why they think it's necessary to educate people that are already here on the company they are visiting, but maybe I'm not alone in not knowing anything about them.

Equi-net has four offices in the metropolitan area and I'm in the Fort Lee version. I didn't pick this one because it's the closest and most convenient, although it certainly is. Instead I picked it because it is where John Lowry was employed when he killed a guy in a bar, with one punch.

Cynthia Warren, the person I'm here to see, is listed as the managing director of the Fort Lee office. She didn't resist at all when I called and in fact seemed intrigued once I mentioned it was Lowry I wanted to talk about.

I'm brought into a conference room with a large table that has sixteen chairs around it. I wasn't expecting such a large crowd, and it turns out that there won't be one. Ms. Warren comes in and closes the door behind her. I have no idea why we're meeting in here; maybe her office is being redecorated, or maybe she's afraid I'll see some secret stock market codes.

Whatever.

She seems pleasant enough, smiling and offering her hand. I've already been asked by the receptionist if I want anything to drink, but Warren offers again. Then we sit, and I start by asking if she can give me the idiot's version of what Equi-net does.

"We're what is called an ECN. That stands for 'electronic communication network.' The simplest way I can put it is that if you trade stocks, we're one of the places that physically make it happen."

"Do I have a choice where it happens?"

She nods. "Your broker does."

"Why do people use ECNs rather than the other places, whatever the hell they are?"

She smiles. "That's complicated, but very often we manage after-hours trading, and large trades for which the traders would like more privacy than other venues allow."

"By after-hours, you mean when the stock markets are closed? I didn't even know you could do that."

"Oh, yes. It's done all the time, more every year. Everything is done by computer, of course, and it is all virtually instantaneous. But essentially if you want to buy a stock at a certain price, we match your request with someone who wants to sell that stock at the same price. Simple as that."

"I suspect it's more complicated than that."

She nods. "For us, but not for you. Do you have a brokerage account?"

"No, but I have a checking account. I don't like to brag, but I get free checking."

She laughs. "Congratulations. But let's say you had an online brokerage account. You input the trade you want to make, hoping and assuming that somebody will be on the other side of that trade. So you press the button, and by the time you refresh your screen, it's done."

"How do you make your money?"

"We get a fee, a very small fee, for every transaction."

"So it doesn't matter to you if the market goes up or down?"

"Not in terms of our revenue. All we want is high volume."

"Tell me about John Lowry."

"Ah, John Lowry. A major disappointment to me, professionally and personally." She actually looks and sounds saddened by the situation; clearly she had expected better from Lowry.

"How so?"

"He is a brilliant IT guy; maybe the best I've ever seen. Our computer systems are literally our lifeblood, and having him here was a wonderful security blanket. He is also very cool in a crisis, and it seems like we have one every day. We've missed him."

"You said you miss him personally as well?"

She nods. "Yes. I liked John, as did everyone here. He is a team player and fun to have around. The kind of person you can count on."

"So you would take him back when he gets out?"

She thinks for a moment. "I would personally, but I doubt I could get it approved by management. He's a felon; in fact he killed someone. Not a great thing to have on your résumé." Then, "You know, the ironic thing is he was trying to help a woman who was being abused."

I don't think I'll mention that, according to Andy, the woman may herself be a murder victim. "So there is nothing that Lowry did here that caused you concern?"

"What kind of concern?"

"I don't know; I'm fishing here."

"You're not going to catch anything. Nothing that he did concerned me."

"Did he have contact with clients? The people making trades?"

She nods. "Some of the larger ones. When there were computer and programming issues to be resolved."

I take a shot. "What about Miles Sloane?"

She nods. "Oh. Miles is a very good client. I can't answer specifically, but I wouldn't be at all surprised if John had contact with Miles, or at least with his company."

Now that is interesting.

I'M NOT CLOSE TO SAYING THAT ALL THE PIECES ARE FALLING INTO PLACE. It would be more accurate to say that we might be starting to identify pieces that are connected and might someday fall into place. Or not.

The center of our universe, at the moment, is Miles Sloane. His estranged ex-partner, Drew Lockman, was tried and acquitted in Judge Henderson's courtroom. Andy Carpenter thought Henderson's charge to the jury was questionable and most probably helped secure the acquittal.

Sloane admitted that he hired the now-deceased Kevin Vickers for various assignments and was paying him a retainer. While following Judge Henderson, Vickers called Sloane at his company on three different occasions.

Lastly, John Lowry, who was also convicted in Judge Henderson's courtroom and who is seeking a retrial, was connected through business to Sloane. To represent him he also employed

Walter Cummings, a lawyer who Lowry is unlikely to have been able to afford on his own.

Each of these things could conceivably be dismissed as coincidences, if coincidences existed in my business. They don't and never have.

So we could be said to be making progress, though even that is not a certainty. What is definite is that we can't come close to answering a large list of questions right now, but all contain elements that are highly suspicious.

For instance, did Judge Henderson interfere inappropriately to get Drew Lockman acquitted? If so, who paid him? Lockman was by then cut loose by his partner and was a pariah among the investors, like Arthur McKnight, who believed Lockman bilked them. And if someone did pay Henderson off, and he complied, why did they seek revenge against him? Or did they pay him to convict Lockman, and he turned on his benefactors?

Next, what does John Lowry have to do with this? Is his computer expertise so essential to someone that they desperately want to secure his freedom? How could he be that important to Sloane or anyone else?

Also, after spending so much time and money to get incriminating evidence against Henderson, why were the blackmailers so quick to give up and release that evidence to the public? They gave him twenty-four hours to change his mind, but gave the information to CNN before that clock even started ticking.

Most bizarrely, what does Luis Valdez have to do with any of this? We have concrete evidence that the blackmailers wanted him to beat the murder charges against him, but why? There seems to be no logical connection between Valdez and that high-powered investment world.

But possibly the effort to get Luis off is not about Luis, but rather a way to appease Renny. Could the blackmailers need Renny and his gang? Why would they?

This has to be about money; the two other traditional motives, power and sex, don't seem to apply. So what could these kind of people, who seem to already have substantial wealth, be involved with that would earn them the kind of money worth doing all this for?

Only two things to sell come to mind, drugs and arms. Maybe Renny's gang is essential to what the blackmailers are doing in this area; maybe they're providing people and/or muscle. I just don't see why the X Gang would be necessary; for the right money there unfortunately is no shortage of people like that to hire.

I call Laurie to relate my conversation with Cynthia Warren about John Lowry. She obviously doesn't have answers to the questions I've raised and, in fact, adds another one. Why did it take eighteen months for the blackmailers to come forward? They started putting money in the Caymans account long ago; it wasn't necessary to delay this long to make their point. And the Eva Staley hotel photograph was taken back at the origin of all this too.

Whatever they were hoping to accomplish could have happened six months or even a year ago, so why wait?

"We need to put Sam on Sloane and his company," Laurie says. "To see if there is anything unusual going on."

"Laurie . . ."

"I'm talking about publicly available records. That will be the first thing he looks into."

"And if he doesn't find anything there?"

"Then I think he should look further. I know we don't agree about this, and believe it or not, when I have these conversations with Andy, I take the other side. Your side. But I think the ends justify the means here, and if I'm wrong, I'm prepared to live with that."

I'm not going to be able to talk her out of it, and I'm not sure if I want to. I trust ourselves not to do any harm with any information we collect, and if it helps us nail blackmailers and murderers, it's a good trade-off.

I can feel myself crossing over to the dark side.

ELLIS KNEW HE WAS TAKING A CHANCE BY VISITING JOHN LOWRY IN PRISON. His employers had attempted to insulate him from any contact with Lowry, or even knowing about him. He only learned about Lowry and his essential involvement with the conspiracy because of the wiretaps in Boston and Philadelphia. But his visiting Lowry could conceivably become known to them, if they were smart enough to have the proper surveillance in place.

Ellis was betting that they weren't smart enough, at least as it related to these matters. They were people of wealth, whose idea of slumming it was to go to a charity dinner where they served chicken. They weren't comfortable in this world, but Ellis had lived here all his life.

He took all the precautions he could. He created a fake ID, another of his specialties, to represent himself as a lawyer in Walter Cummings's firm, merely coming to consult with Lowry, their client. Not only would this conceal his real identity, but it would allow them to meet in a private room, supposedly free of recording devices.

Ellis did not trust the prison authorities not to listen in, so he resolved to talk cryptically, but in a way that Lowry would understand. Lowry had no way of knowing that he was about to participate in the most important conversation of his life.

They met in a prison anteroom; Ellis was waiting when Lowry was brought in. Ellis was surprised by Lowry's size and obvious good physical shape, though it fit with his being in prison for killing a man with one punch.

Lowry seemed surprised to see someone that he didn't recognize. "Who are you?"

"It doesn't matter who I am; what matters is what I have to say."

"Okay, what do you have to say?"

"One way or another, you're going to be getting out of here very soon. The people that are working on your behalf, your future employers, are very powerful, the types who get what they want."

"Sounds good to me."

"Would you rather be a partner than an employee?"

"What does mean?"

"I'm talking carefully here because you never know who might be listening. But nothing happens without you; everyone else can be replaced, you can't. Without you they have nothing."

Lowry nods. "So?"

"Come on, you know how valuable that makes you?"

"I'm going to do fine."

"Bullshit. It's a lot compared to what you've made in the past. It's nothing compared to what you can make if you play this right."

"Keep talking." Lowry appeared suddenly to show real interest.

"You know the money they pay pro athletes, and how everybody complains about it. They're paying backup shortstops ten million a year. Top guys are getting thirty. You know why? Because they bring in people and they make money for the owners. The owners are not giving the money away; they pay because that way they can make even more. The players literally make the big money because they are worth the big money."

"Okay . . ."

"John, you are the star quarterback, Cy Young Award winner, and NBA MVP all wrapped into one. They need you or they have nothing." Then Ellis dropped the bomb. "And when they don't need you anymore, you'll be found floating in the river. Believe me, I know."

Lowry shook his head. "Not true. I know the code. That's why I haven't given it to them; this way they have to get me out. They'll never stop needing me."

Ellis sighed, as if saddened by what he was hearing. "John, you don't have any idea what or who you are dealing with. Give me a half hour alone in a room with you, and not only will you give up the code, you'll give up your mother. Trust me on this; I do their dirty work, so I know who they are. They will try and get rid of me as well; that's why I'm here."

Lowry was shaken by what he heard; the intensity and quiet coldness in Ellis's voice and demeanor impressed and scared him. "Where do you fit in?"

Ellis smiled. "I fit like a glove. Because like you, I have the knowledge."

"You don't know anything about it."

"I know that it exists, and what it does. I can leave here,

make one anonymous phone call to a reporter, or to the FBI, and it's all over. They'd come in and shut it down, because the only way it works is in the dark. You understand? I make that phone call and they have nothing. They don't make a dime and you rot in here."

"I need time to think."

Ellis smiled and stood up. "No problem; this is an important decision. But the day you walk out of here is the day you have to make it. And, John, if you mention this conversation to anyone, ever . . . if you talk about it in your sleep or write it in your diary . . . well, that would be a major mistake from which you would never recover."

"I understand."

"Good. Welcome to the big time."

Ellis left the prison pleased with the results of the conversation. He already had the leverage of knowing what was going on, but having Lowry on his side increased that leverage exponentially.

He would not have been so pleased if he knew that he was being watched.

"THERE IS A LIMIT TO WHAT WE CAN KNOW IN A SITUATION LIKE THIS."

That's how Sam Willis begins his presentation on Miles Sloane and his company. Sam continues, "I can tell you the facts, but not how they came about. For example, I can tell you how he came into some money, but not necessarily why he was given it, or what he had to promise in return."

"Understood," Laurie says. She, Marcus, and I are sitting with Sam around Andy's conference table as Sam talks. To call it a "conference table" might be giving it too much credit; it would have trouble hosting a bridge game if the participants were overweight.

"So I have personal information on Sloane as well as his business, though there seems not to be much separation between the two. The business is privately owned; his ex-partner Drew Lockman still owns a piece, but Sloane easily has controlling interest."

"Is everything you learned publicly available?" I know the

answer to the question clearly is no, and I'm asking only to be obnoxious.

Sam looks surprised and unsure as he looks at Laurie for help. None seems to be forthcoming, so he answers by saying, "Well, it depends on your definition of publicly available."

"I didn't know there were different definitions," I say. "But just to be clear, by *publicly available,* I mean 'available to the public.'"

Sam hesitates. "Well, I'm a member of the public, and it was available to me."

"Please continue, Sam," Laurie says.

"Okay. My estimate would be that Sloane has a net worth of five and a half million dollars. That includes a house that's probably good for two million in Alpine, three cars, and a portfolio of equities. His own portfolio is obviously managed by his own company. I can tell you what stocks he owns; there's a lot of tech and energy, but I doubt it's important."

"It's not," I say. I'm surprised that Sloane's net worth is not higher, though at $5.5 million he probably has me beat by close to $5.5 million. It's all relative. Sloane told me that Arthur McKnight's money begins with a *b,* but Sloane's begins with an *m* . . . the poor guy.

Sam continues, "The company is essentially an asset manager, meaning that people give them money to invest and they make decisions, based on the strategy that they've agreed upon with the clients. They also do brokerage work, but that's not their primary function. Currently they are managing a little over six hundred million."

"Do you know whose money they are managing?" Laurie asks.

Sam nods. "Yes. It's all in the folders I gave you, as is everything else I'm saying. It's a little dry, so I'm trying to give you the highlights."

"What's the biggest highlight? What surprised you, if anything?"

"Oh, something definitely surprised me, and I think you might find it very interesting. It involves money sent to the company, though I can't be sure why it was sent. I know it was received, but it could have been for investment purposes or even to buy a small share in the company. Hard to tell, but I'm still trying."

"Don't they get money coming in all the time?" I ask.

Sam shakes his head. "Not as often as you think. Most of the clients are long-term players, so sometimes they will take money in and out, but not frequently."

"So why was this money surprising?"

"It came from eight different companies, all first-time clients of Sloane. Each of them sent in a million five, all eight, the exact amount."

Laurie nods. "That is strange."

"It gets stranger. The eight companies are all privately owned brokerages, not very different from Sloane's. Not necessarily competitors, because they're located all over the country, but they are giving Sloane money most likely to do what they already do."

"And all the same amounts," I say. "So it can't possibly be a coincidence. Did Sloane do the same for them? Did he send any of them money?"

"If he did, I don't see it."

"When did the money come in?"

"Over a very long time; the first came in twenty-one months ago, and the last just six weeks ago. No activity involving those companies since."

Laurie turns to me. "Any ideas?"

"It almost seems like an initiation fee of some sort, since it's a onetime payment."

Laurie nods. "I agree. Or dues. But it feels like they were joining a club."

"A club with more than enough money to blackmail Judge Henderson," I say. Then, "So let's assume, and I recognize it's a big assumption, that we have now found our conspirators, or at least some of them. We still don't know what they are trying to accomplish, or whether John Lowry connects to them. And if he does, how?"

"Can't answer that," Laurie says, then smiles. "But we're making progress."

IT WOULD BE HARD TO IMAGINE A MORE ANTICLIMACTIC EVENT THAN THE Luis Valdez trial.

Word had gotten out, as word is wont to do, about the circumstances leading up to the death of Judge Henderson. Included in those leaked revelations was the connection to Valdez and the pressure that Henderson was under to make a ruling that could get him off.

That immediately ratcheted up the notoriety of the case from zero to sixty. Which in turn resulted in a packed gallery and ramped-up security. Valdez, who had been mostly anonymous in the pretrial run-up, was suddenly a name familiar to everyone.

The public weren't sure why they were interested in Valdez, but they were paying rapt attention. Gruesome details of the murders he was alleged to have committed surfaced, and conspiracy theories pointing to his being framed gained viral traction.

Judge Robert Pletka was presiding. Having taken over as

acting chief judge, Pletka was intent on taking the controversial case for himself. He didn't want to dump it on one of the other judges; he spoke about how that would not be right. People speculated that in doing so Judge Pletka was showing the kind of leadership that would result in his permanent appointment as top judge.

The intense interest in the case also led to media focus on the X Gang, and Paterson's gang situation in general. The gangs didn't desire the attention as demands grew for increased police pressure on them. Renny Valdez in particular was a subject of media focus, both because of his gang leadership and his being the brother of the infamous Luis Valdez.

Then came the trial.

It lasted all of forty-eight hours. Richard Wallace, the lead prosecutor assigned to the case, had ample evidence, both forensic and eyewitness. He presented it thoroughly and efficiently, leaving little room for the defense to maneuver. They only called two witnesses in presenting their case, neither of whom had any impact on the jury.

Judge Pletka, who had prepared for any and all eventualities, had an easy time of it. His charge to the jury was straight and to the point; it was by the book and clearly immune to any appeal challenges later on.

The jurors took a little over a day to reach a verdict. It would have gone even faster had they not been reacting to the significant public interest. They felt they might be missing something, that if people were in such an uproar about it, there must be more to it.

So they went overboard in discussing it, both to be fair and to not look to the outside world like they were giving it short shrift. They wanted to be diligent and, just as important, to look diligent.

Finally they informed the judge that they had reached a verdict, and the public waited. Not with bated breath; only those who hadn't been following the trial were not positive about the outcome. Everyone else had no doubt as to how it would end, and they were proven correct.

Luis Valdez was guilty as charged.

Twenty-four hours later, nobody cared and everyone barely remembered.

IN A WAY, AN INVESTIGATOR IS LIKE AN NFL RUNNING BACK.

Of course, there are differences between investigators like me and the Saquon Barkleys and Ezekiel Elliotts of the world. We make a fraction of the money, have none of the glory, and usually don't get the girl.

But we are alike in one area crucial to both jobs: We are always faced with one key decision. Go head-on or go around. When a running back in the open field approaches a potential tackler, he has to decide whether to go around him or try to run over him. There is simply no other way to do it, no third choice.

Detectives face the same choice in approaching a subject, or a person of interest. Do you go around him and try to learn what you can, or do you go the confrontation route and go at him directly? The answer for both us and the running back obviously depends on the situation, and how much we need to gain.

We know that a group of at least eight people, each a wealthy businessman operating in the world of finance, made a strange investment of a million and a half dollars to Miles Sloane's company. We don't know why, and we have no obvious way of finding out.

Which would seem to rule out the indirect approach.

The direct approach carries its own disadvantages. Most obviously, if we confront one of the eight men, then he and they will know they are being investigated and that we have knowledge of the transactions. Our assumption is that they are so far unaware of that, since the only way we learned about it was to have Sam Willis conduct his online investigation. We have an advantage in the suspects' not knowing what we know, and by speaking to them directly we give that up. And once we give that secret up, there is no getting it back.

But there is definitely an alternative view of this. It's not that the person will break down and confess to some nefarious deed, but we will get to see the person's reaction when surprised by the revelation. The person will also have a response, concocted either in advance or in the moment, and that response will put the person on record.

So after a team strategy session, we have decided to go at it directly. The two closest people on the list of investors are Gerald Stidham, in Boston, and Donald Crossland, in Philadelphia. I will take Stidham and Laurie will deal with Crossland.

Getting in to see Stidham was a breeze. Shocking as it may seem, money talks, even if you only claim to have some. I called and told Stidham I was looking to make a large investment, in the $30 million range, and that he came highly recommended.

He asked me questions, which I deflected by telling him that I preferred talking in person. He agreed, probably on the theory that large money might be made on the upside, while the downside to meeting me was simply wasting a few minutes of his time.

I had the option of taking a train up here but decided instead to drive. I like to be in control and not subject to schedules, delays, and cancellations, though obviously New York–Boston traffic is clearly beyond my control.

I'm in Stidham's Back Bay office about to drop the bomb. He seems relaxed and confident, smooth on the edge of smarmy, as we sit down in his office, coffee in hand. "So what can I do for you?" he asks.

"You can tell me why you sent Miles Sloane a million and a half dollars last year."

People will often say that when someone is shocked, the color drains out of their face, but I've surprised a lot of people in my work, and I've never seen it happen. I've always thought it was just an expression, an exaggeration at best and total bullshit at worst.

Until now. The color has just drained out of Gerald Stidham's face.

"What is this?"

"If you're talking about what I just said, it was a question, and a fairly simple one. To recap, I asked why you sent Miles Sloane a million and a half dollars."

"Who are you?"

"I'm a private investigator working on a case involving Miles Sloane. You are not a suspect in any wrongdoing, even though my sense is that you are in the process of acting like one."

"You're here under false pretenses."

"No question about it. Now what's your answer?"

"I don't have to talk to you."

I nod. "No question about that either. But here's the way it works. I just finished twenty-five years as a police officer. If I don't get answers to my questions, I'll get some of my old buddies to ask them. And they won't come here under false pretenses;

they'll drag your ass down to the station and keep asking until you answer."

Pretty much everything I just said after the "twenty-five years" part is total crap. I was a New Jersey cop; they're not coming up here to Boston to question anybody. And if they did, they wouldn't drag him to the station; in real life he'd get a lawyer and force them to back off. But guys like Stidham have no experience whatsoever in this kind of stuff. Even when they are criminals, they don't see themselves that way. So they get scared. Right now Stidham is scared.

"I make a lot of investments. That was just one of many."

I nod. "I see. I'm going to assume that when you make each one of those investments, you have a reason for doing so. What was your reason for making that one?"

"To make money. Sloane is very good at these things."

"Better than you? Because you're in the same business."

"He uses different strategies. Sometimes they work, sometimes not. Nothing is foolproof in this business. None of us has a patent on investment techniques that work. So we try and diversify."

"Any other examples of similar attempts at diversity you've tried in the past with other, similar companies?"

"That is proprietary information which is, quite frankly, none of your business."

Stidham is recovering his composure. I'm not going to get anything more out of him other than the garbage he has already spewed. But that's okay; I learned what I needed to learn from his reaction. The million and a half he gave to Sloane was no ordinary investment.

Now we need to figure out why he made it.

ONCE I'M HOME, LAURIE AND I COMPARE NOTES.

She is just back from her meeting in Philadelphia with Crossland, and she grilled him in the same manner that I did, since we had planned it all out in advance.

Once I describe how Stidham reacted, she said, "I had the identical experience with Crossland. He panicked when he found out I was not there to give him money, and it wasn't because I was not there to give him money."

"Did he answer the question?"

"Again, just like you. He tried to get out of it at first, but eventually he claimed it was just another investment because Sloane was good at getting money to make money. He said that he didn't have a patent on investment techniques."

"Bingo. That was the exact sentence that Stidham used. They obviously were coached on what to say if they were confronted. Fortunately they didn't also get acting lessons."

Laurie says, "These were not just ordinary investments. These guys did not want them to be known, and they do not want to say why they made them. Which is to say they are extraordinarily shady."

"So now they know that we know, and soon their bosses will know. The question is what they will do about it. One thing is for sure, they are not going to fold up their tents and go home. Not with all that they've put into it."

"Do you realize how much money must be at stake here? Forget the account in the Caymans. These eight people put up twelve million dollars, and that's just to gain admission to the club. You can be sure they're not looking to make five percent on their money."

"They could come after us. Be careful; maybe Marcus should be watching out for you."

"What about you?"

"I've got Simon."

She laughs. "I've got Andy and Tara."

"Like I said, Marcus should be watching out for you."

With that not even close to settled, the conversation turns to John Lowry and what his involvement with this conspiracy might be. "He's not a money guy, that's for sure," I say. "It has to be because of his computer expertise; Cynthia Warren at Equi-net told me he's the best."

"So whatever they are doing involves computer crime, and Lowry is the key. They need him out of prison to get it done. So why were they focused on Luis Valdez?"

"I've been thinking about that a lot. I don't think they were; I think Valdez was a head fake. They were using him to see if Henderson would give in to their demands. If he did, then they would reveal that Lowry was their real goal. If he didn't, then they could go to plan B with us thinking that it was about Valdez. It was smart, and we fell for it."

"That's for sure."

"Does Andy have an opinion on whether Lowry will get the new trial?"

"He thinks it's more likely than not, considering the missing witness and the possible judicial error in Henderson's charge to the jury. The real question in his mind is whether or not they will let Lowry out on bail while he awaits trial. Judge Pletka is handling the case, and Andy says he's almost as much of a hard-ass as Henderson."

"If they do, they will never see him again. The guys he's working for will spend whatever is necessary to make him disappear to a place where only they have access. They'll put him in the Criminals Protection Program."

"You think we should confront him?" Laurie asks.

"Not yet; we need to see how this plays out for a little while. We can always go that route. When is the hearing?"

"Tomorrow morning. Andy is going to be there."

"So am I," I say. "Right now I have nothing else to do."

RADOSLAV DURIC HAD NO TROUBLE GETTING THROUGH US CUSTOMS IN Philadelphia.

His fake identification was, not surprisingly, perfectly prepared, the best that money could buy.

All he brought with him was a carry-on bag; he would not be in the country long and always traveled light. So within forty-five minutes of touching down, he was in the car being driven to New Jersey.

Duric considered it silly that he had been instructed to fly to Philadelphia, when that was not where his assignment was. He assumed his employers, whom he had never met, were just extra-cautious. So Duric accepted that decision; they were paying the bills.

Duric was also a bit surprised that they did not have someone local who could handle this. It was not going to be difficult; he could manage it in his sleep. But people with this kind of money can go to great lengths and great cost to make sure things are done exactly right, and they made a good choice in Duric.

He was quite literally a hired gun, and if there was a better one in the world, Duric was not aware of him.

So Duric was taken to a hotel, where he checked in under the same fake name he used to travel and enter the country. He would wait there; the expectation was that it would not be more than a few days.

Then he would do the job he had traveled so far to do. Unless some other lucrative assignment emerged, he would then go home.

He would be much wealthier than when he arrived.

THE LOWRY HEARING STANDS IN MARKED CONTRAST TO ALL THE EXCITE-ment over the Luis Valdez trial.

There has been no publicity, no media attention whatsoever, and the public seems to be totally unaware of it. The gallery is virtually empty; Andy and I represent a third of the entire crowd. I don't know who the other four people are, but I surreptitiously take their pictures with my iPhone, just in case they are involved in our case.

The only similarity, other than its being in the same courtroom as Valdez, is the presiding judge, Robert Pletka. I'm sure that the reason Pletka kept this case for himself is that it involves a claim of judicial error by Judge Henderson. That would make it a likely candidate for scrutiny in the Office of Judicial Ethics' investigation of Henderson's cases, so Pletka would want to make sure it is conducted strictly by the book.

Pletka had conducted an initial hearing in the case and

directed the parties to have their briefs filed and arguments ready for today.

Lowry sits at the defense table with Walter Cummings, who probably charges as much by the hour as Lowry used to make by the week. Norman Trell, a career prosecutor and, according to Andy, a competent one, is representing the county.

Pletka is a no-nonsense judge, which I am pleased about since I've been in court for ten minutes and I'm bored to death. He gets right to it. "Gentlemen, I've read the briefs, so talk to me. Mr. Cummings?"

"Thank you, Your Honor. Mr. Lowry has been incarcerated for seventeen months for a crime that the jury should never have even considered. To make matters worse, not only were they directed to consider it, but Judge Henderson failed to educate them on the nature of the crime in his charge.

"As Your Honor knows, intentional manslaughter includes with it the knowledge of the perpetrator that his actions would result in death. Judge Henderson did not tell the jury this uncontested fact, though he was required to do so. The prosecution would have you believe that Mr. Lowry should have anticipated his victim's demise because of his career as a professional boxer.

"Mr. Lowry won twelve of his twenty fights, four by knockouts. In none of those fights did his opponents suffer serious injury, nor did any of them die. He no doubt threw hundreds if not thousands of punches in those fights, and at the time he was younger and more powerful. For him to believe that this single punch would result in death is simply silly and not at all supported by the facts or common logic.

"The fact is that if he was guilty of anything at all, and we deny that he is, then it is reckless manslaughter. As you know, Your Honor, conviction on that count would be a much lesser offense and would result in a much lesser punishment.

"So we ask for a new trial, so that Mr. Lowry can be vindicated entirely. In the meantime, he should be released on his own recognizance, since his time served would be very likely to already exceed any punishment on the lesser offense.

"Simple justice demands that he be allowed to go home today to resume his productive life. Thank you, Your Honor."

Pletka turns to the prosecution table. "Mr. Trell?"

"Your Honor, as you know, to consider the judicial error serious enough to warrant a mistrial, you must find that it is more likely than not that it would have changed the outcome. That is clearly not the case here. There was testimony during the trial about how boxers are trained to be extra-cautious and to avoid fighting outside the ring at all costs.

"They absolutely know what can happen in such a circumstance, which is entirely different from the action within the four corners of the boxing ring. Mr. Cummings is being disingenuous when he compares the two. For one thing, in a professional fight the person being punched is always a trained fighter himself, but far more important is the obvious fact that boxers in the ring wear padded gloves.

"Those gloves are worn to protect against serious damage and death. Every boxer knows this; in fact, every person knows this. Certainly the jury knew it, and they were aware that Mr. Lowry knew it as well. Judge Henderson stating the obvious would have changed nothing.

"We believe that no action is warranted here, Your Honor."

"Thank you. There is a mention made in the brief of a missing witness? Maria Burks? Why did you not speak to that?"

"Your Honor, there was no reason to speak to it because it is not relevant," Trell says. "The witness was available during the trial and testified freely and completely. There is no need for us to keep track of witnesses long after the trial has taken place."

"Nevertheless, can you describe the facts as you know them?"

"My knowledge isn't complete, but Ms. Burks left the area and moved to Ohio soon after the trial. She was there for a few months and then disappeared. I do not know the circumstances behind the disappearance, but the police there are treating it as a missing person's case, with the possibility of foul play.

"As I said, it should have no bearing on these proceedings; her testimony is in the record and is unchallenged."

Pletka turns to Cummings, who is all too willing to jump on this. "Your Honor, it is clearly relevant. Should Your Honor grant us the mistrial, as is warranted in this matter, Ms. Burks's unavailability would be determinative: without her testimony they have no case. In addition to all that I mentioned previously, Mr. Lowry should not remain incarcerated when there is no possibility of another conviction. Without her the prosecution would be committing legal malpractice even to retry the case."

Pletka asks a few more questions, but nothing more of real consequence is discussed. He thanks the counsel and says that he will consider the matter and likely issue an order on Friday, which is two days away. The order will be posted on the court website.

My view is that Cummings's arguments carried the day, and that Lowry will get the new trial. I have no idea if he will get bail. I'm interested in hearing Andy's opinion; he's obviously more knowledgeable about these things than I am.

I don't have to wait long. No sooner has Pletka banged his gavel to end the hearing than Andy says, "Lowry might as well pack his toothbrush. He's going home on Friday."

COREY DOUGLAS WAS WRONG.

He had been certain that once he and Laurie confronted Stidham and Crossland about their investments with Miles Sloane, they would immediately turn around and alert the other conspirators, including their bosses, to what had happened.

They did not.

They talked to each other, and only each other, about what had happened. Both expressed surprise that the other was also contacted. They speculated as to whether the other six investors were also questioned, but did not know any of them well enough to ask.

Stidham and Crossland knew little; they didn't even know if this investigation into Sloane related to their operation. Maybe Sloane had done something else worth investigating, unrelated to what they were involved in. Maybe they were just questioned because they had made the investments.

They decided to keep their interviews with the investigators to themselves. This came from a combination of fear and greed. They feared that to make the revelation might result in the organizers considering them radioactive. That would result in their removal from the group.

That's where the greed came in. Right now they were branches of an incredible money tree, and they did not want to be cut off when the time was getting close. They had waited too long.

But while the two men came to the same decision not to disclose the investigative interviews, they did not realize that in the moment they were doing exactly that.

Ellis, who had installed the wiretaps on them to learn what the operational details were, had not removed them. He believed that he might in time learn more helpful information, a belief that proved prophetic.

His first reaction was surprise. The investigators were obviously the ones who had been hired by Judge Henderson. Ellis had assumed they would stand down once their client was dead, but they had not.

They would have to be dealt with, but that would wait until later.

For now, Ellis had other things on his plate.

I THOUGHT SOME MORE ABOUT JOHN LOWRY, WHICH LED ME TO CALL CYNTHIA Warren.

The only thing we had to connect Lowry to Miles Sloane was his employment at Equi-net, the company that physically made stock trades on their servers. Warren, Lowry's immediate supervisor at the New Jersey office, confirmed that Lowry and people at Sloane's company would definitely have had contact. The connection seemed too obvious to ignore, or to write off as a potential coincidence.

She was helpful last time, and I'm hoping she will be again. "Ms. Warren, I've got just a couple more questions so I can wrap up my investigation."

"Happy to help if I can."

"Great. Would John Lowry have had contact with clients, brokerage companies and the like, that were out of town?"

"What do you mean by 'out of town'?"

"Places like Boston, Philadelphia, Atlanta . . ."

She interrupts, laughing, before I can continue, "I'm sorry, I thought by 'out of town' you might have meant outside of Fort Lee. The answer is definitely not. John worked locally."

This is disappointing and somewhat surprising. "Are you sure?"

"I'm positive."

"I would have thought that trades can come in from anywhere, since it's all done on computer."

"That's certainly true; we handle trades that come in from all over the world. But we are talking about IT issues; John would almost never have to be at a different physical location to deal with those kind of things."

"I see."

"Is there anything else you want to know?"

I decide to go at it from another angle. "You said that Sloane Enterprises is a frequent trader on your servers."

"That's correct."

"If I mention some other companies, can you tell me if the same thing is true for them?"

"Sure. None of this is confidential information."

I read off the list of eight companies that invested $1.5 million in Sloane Enterprises, though I don't tell her why I picked those eight. She writes them down and asks me to hold while she checks her records. It takes about five minutes for her to return.

"Sorry to keep you waiting. Yes, all eight companies are clients."

Bingo. "Ms. Warren, when it comes to these types of companies, what percentage of them, speaking nationally, would you say trade on your servers?"

"Well, we're actually fairly small for this industry, and we have many competitors. I don't know exactly, but I would say somewhere between five and ten percent?"

I spend a few moments letting the impact of what she just said sink in. I was not a math major in college, and my knowledge of statistics pretty much begins with earned run averages and ends with yards per carry. But I do know that when I get eight out of eight positives on something for which the average is between 5 and 10 percent, that falls well outside the laws of probability.

"Mr. Douglas?"

"Sorry . . . I was thinking about what you just said. I'm going to tell you something which you are going to be disinclined to believe, but please take it seriously."

"What is it?"

"These companies that I just mentioned are going to attempt to exploit your system, unethically and illegally, to realize great profits that they do not deserve. On some level, and I don't know how, John Lowry is involved."

Now it's her turn to spend a few quiet moments. "Mr. Douglas, I will speak to our systems and IT people about this, but it is simply not possible. We facilitate trades, we make no decisions about them. Willing buyers and sellers are simply matched together, and the price is the price. If one side were to profit unfairly, the other side would be unfairly damaged. No traders would tolerate that."

"I understand what you're saying. I would suggest two things. One, that you do as you said and review this with your people. Two, and this is very important, if John Lowry contacts you, either looking for his job back or to somehow be involved in your business, you should call me immediately. It will then be time to bring in the authorities."

"I will do that."

I get off the phone certain of two things: the answer is clearly at Equi-net, and it all revolves around John Lowry.

JUDGE ROBERT PLETKA POSTED HIS RULING, AS PROMISED, ON THE COURT website. It was one page long.

John Lowry's conviction for intentional manslaughter was overturned, due to the jury's not being properly informed as to the exact circumstances necessary to prove guilt. Implicit in this area of the opinion was a rebuke of Judge Henderson for his charge to the jury not mentioning that intentional manslaughter requires an understanding by the perpetrator that death was a likely outcome of his actions.

Reading between the not very subtle lines, Judge Pletka was authorizing a retrial, but was not in favor of the prosecution's proceeding with one. Lowry had spent a year and a half in prison, and it seemed obvious that Pletka considered that punishment ample for the crime.

He didn't stop there. He granted Lowry's request for bail, pending the prosecution's decision about a retrial. Bail was set at a minimal $25,000, a sure indication that Pletka believed Lowry should not spend another day behind bars.

The net effect was clear: Lowry would be a free man that afternoon.

A number of people had waited for that announcement for a long time. The one person who had not been waiting that long was the one planning to take immediate action.

John Lowry and Ellis had not been in contact since Ellis paid him a visit in prison and made his offer to form a partnership. The offer on the table was to use the obvious leverage Lowry had as the technical brains behind the conspiracy to extract far more money than they were currently due.

Ellis also had his own leverage; he could threaten to reveal the scheme to the authorities. But with Lowry on his side, the pressure could be ratcheted up considerably. Ellis had the potential power to expose and kill the operation; Lowry was its very lifeline.

So Ellis headed for the prison immediately upon hearing the news. He knew he would get there earlier than necessary; bail would have to be arranged, paperwork done, and the information communicated to prison officials. Nothing the bureaucracy got its hands on went smoothly.

But that was okay; Ellis would wait as long as it took.

Not until past six o'clock did Lowry come walking through the door; he looked up at the sky as if savoring his freedom. Ellis smiled to himself; he thought released prisoners only did that in movies.

With Lowry was Walter Cummings, his attorney and the man most responsible for his release, unless one wanted to give more credit to the people who had paid Cummings. In any case, Cummings had delivered, leaving Lowry free to look up at the sky.

They got into Cummings's Lexus and drove off, with Ellis

following. He had no intention of approaching Lowry with Cummings present, so he figured he might be in for another wait. For all he knew, attorney and client might be going out to dinner.

They were not. Cummings dropped Lowry off at his house in Lodi. Ellis wasn't surprised that Lowry had kept the house while he was in prison; the people that could afford Cummings could afford Lowry's mortgage payments. They could also obviously afford a gardener; the grass was neatly trimmed. Ellis was sure that Lowry's car must be in the garage, probably recently tuned and filled with gas.

Lowry got out of the car and took another look at the sky, which probably wasn't that different from the sky above the prison. He went around the side and opened the garage door to confirm that his car was, in fact, there. It was.

He went inside and turned on some lights. Ellis looked around to make sure no one was watching, then went to the front door and rang the bell.

Lowry answered the door and didn't seem surprised to see Ellis standing there. "That was fast. Come in."

They went into the kitchen and Lowry opened the refrigerator. "I'd offer you something to eat or drink, but I don't have anything to eat or drink."

"Have you thought about my proposal?"

"Of course. What else did I have to do?"

"Are you in, or out?"

Lowry waited a few beats before answering. "How much do we ask them for?"

Ellis successfully tried to avoid smiling. "We don't ask, we tell."

"Fair enough." Lowry smiled at the prospect. "So how much?"

"Fifty percent. Twenty-five for you, twenty-five for me, fifty for them. They are putting up the money."

"Sounds good to me. They let me rot there for seventeen months while they set the whole thing up."

"You realize that once you're in, you're in all the way."

Lowry nodded. "Yes, I understand that."

"I'll set up a meeting so we can drop the bomb on them."

"You think they'll go for it?"

"Do they need you?"

"Without me they've got nothing. They'd be spinning their wheels."

"Good. Try and keep that in mind, because they know that as well as you do."

DANI SAID SOMETHING LAST NIGHT THAT GOT ME THINKING.

We were talking on the phone, which for me is by itself something of a news event. I hate talking on the phone; I don't know why, but it has always felt awkward to me. At every pause in the conversation, I use it as an excuse to get off.

But with Dani it's different. It's comfortable and the conversation flows easily. Last night we talked for more than a half hour. We haven't seen each other much lately; both of our jobs have gotten in the way. I'm finding that I'm missing her, a sensation I am not familiar with.

We were trying to find a time to get together, and she said that Friday wasn't good, that she was stuck going to a black-tie charity dinner for work. I immediately said, "No thanks," even though she hadn't invited me. She started to laugh, and when I asked her why, she said that she would pay good money to see me in a tuxedo, bow tie and all.

That jogged something in my mind, but not until this morning did I figure out what it was. But it is the reason that I am at the Passaic County coroner's office, talking with Janet Carlson, the head of the department.

I told her it was urgent, even though it isn't. I'm just generally in need of instant gratification, and when I have an idea, I need to know right away if it's on target or a load of crap.

Janet is great looking and has a terrific sense of humor; you would never guess in a million years that she chose to cut up dead bodies for a career. I worked with her quite a bit in my former life, and she sent me a nice congratulations card when I retired. Sending cards with handwritten notes is a lost art; not that I have ever done it.

She always seems calm and unhurried; maybe it's because the clients who are in drawers waiting for her aren't in a rush or in a position to complain. So we spend a little time catching up; she knows Laurie well and thinks our forming the team was a great idea.

"We were representing Judge Henderson."

She nods. "I heard that. What a shame for him."

"Actually, in a way we're still representing him. We just want to clear things up, maybe set the record straight."

"I knew him. We weren't close friends or anything, but I knew him well enough that I don't believe he took a bribe for anything."

"Did you ever see him wear a tie?"

She thinks for a moment, then laughs. "No, I don't think I ever did. He even wore an open-collared shirt under his robe. Actually, that sort of surprised me. He was a strict, by-the-book judge, not the casual type at all."

"Yet he hung himself."

"Yes."

"Andy Carpenter said the Judge once told him he hated ties and dress shoes; that his neck and feet needed room to breathe."

"Yes."

"Yet he hung himself."

"Yes," she says for a third time, but softer than the other two. "He did."

"I'm not an expert on suicide, but there are a lot of ways to do it. Especially for a man in his sixties. To make a noose out of wires, attach it to beams so that it holds, climb a ladder, and jump. It seems like a lot of difficult work, when he could have taken pills or gone out to his closed garage and turned on the car. And then you add the fact that he was uncomfortable with anything tight around his neck."

"This is troubling." I think she's talking to herself, trying to mentally fit all of this in with her earlier assessment.

"And no suicide note?"

She shakes her head. "None was found."

"But you were sure it was a suicide?"

"Sure? No, but I had no reason to doubt it. There was a slight bruising on his arm, but nothing serious. No evidence of foul play, no forced entry . . . and it was widely known that the Judge was humiliated and depressed. There was also a sedative in his system, but that would be consistent with him dealing with his high stress level."

"Did he have a prescription for the sedative?"

"I don't know that anyone ever checked; the drug didn't contribute to his death." Then, "Corey, when it comes to a situation like this, one can never be sure what happened. But this seemed like the right call to make."

"And now?"

"Now I don't know. There's still nothing there for me to call it murder."

"But there's no way to know for sure."

She nods, obviously troubled by our conversation. "No way to know for sure. I hope you find out the truth, Corey. The Judge deserves that much."

"Yes, he does."

"I DON'T SEE HOW IT PASSES THE 'WHY' TEST," LAURIE SAYS.

I've just told her my theory about Henderson's death possibly not being a suicide. Her comment about the "why" test means that she has no idea why the blackmailers would have murdered him. We have been failing the "why" test a lot lately.

"Okay, let's play it out," I say. "They had already released the incriminating information about Henderson, so he was no longer of value to them. He had turned them down, told them to kiss his ass . . . maybe they were getting revenge."

"Possible, but it doesn't fit what we think we know about them. They are motivated by money; revenge does nothing for them in that regard."

"They wound up getting what they wanted; Lowry is out of jail."

"Right. And maybe Judge Henderson's death did help them. He had not recused himself; there was no public comment from him about how he was going to handle his upcoming cases. If he kept working, which seemed likely, Lowry would have come before him. He would have been ruling on his own alleged judicial error, which would then have gone to an appeal if he didn't change his ruling."

I nod. "Which would have taken a long time."

"Right. So his death meant the case would go elsewhere; it turned out to be Judge Pletka, but they couldn't have known that."

"It was Pletka's decision where it went; he moved into Henderson's position, so he determines who gets which cases."

"You aren't suggesting that Judge Pletka was on the take?" she asks.

"No. He's got an impeccable reputation."

"As did Judge Henderson."

"True," I say. "But I don't think Henderson did anything wrong. They targeted him, but he didn't give in. But more importantly, they wouldn't have gone after a second judge when Henderson was calling the shots. It's not like Walmart was running a two-for-one judge sale."

"We're getting pretty far afield here simply based on the fact that Judge Henderson didn't like to wear ties. The guy was despondent, and a reputation he had spent an entire life building was crumbling; it's just possible he put aside his fashion sense for once."

"I agree with that. But the suicide always bothered me. Henderson was a tough guy; he prided himself on that. He had no patience for people who were against him. It's hard to picture him giving them a win like that on a silver platter."

"This was about his personal pain," she says. "There is no way to predict what a person in that situation will do. And there's one other thing."

"What's that?"

"The lack of evidence of forced entry. He had a burglar alarm; I saw the code box when we were at his house. He was smart enough not to let somebody in who might cause him harm. But if he was murdered, then that is exactly what he did."

It's hard to refute that, so I don't try. The bottom line is, for our purposes, whether Henderson killed himself or was murdered does not change our approach or mission. We know the blackmailers are capable of murder; they killed Vickers and probably Maria Burks, the witness against Lowry in the bar that night.

Their killing Henderson wouldn't cause us to revise our profile of our enemy, such as it is. We know what they will do to get what they want.

"So where do we go now?" I ask.

"We have two options. We can go to the FBI or the SEC and tell them what we know so far. If there is some kind of financial scam going on, maybe they can stop it."

I interrupt, "I don't think so, at least not yet. We have more suspicions than anything else; there's no way that they would even begin an investigation based on it. Besides, Cynthia Warren at Equi-net is having her tech people look into it now. That would be a first step for anyone. What's the second option?"

"To scare Lowry. To pressure him by making him think we know more than we do. But even if he doesn't believe that, just by confronting him we could make him abandon ship and tell what he knows, if not to us then to the authorities. This is not a hardened criminal; he punched a guy in a bar. He's also not a high-finance guy. He could be willing to just take the fact that he's out of prison and call it a day."

"I would vote for option two. There's not much downside.

Even if Lowry tells us to get lost, we're back where we were. It's not like we're revealing ourselves; the blackmailers have known about us for a long time."

Laurie nods her agreement. "Option two it is."

ELLIS WANTED THIS TO GO RIGHT AND WAS CONFIDENT THAT IT WOULD.

He had called his employers to arrange a meeting, telling them that he had learned something important that would benefit them to know. He was pressed to indicate what it was, but said that it was not something to be said on a phone line that might not be secure.

So the meeting was set at a cabin just west of Parsippany. The employer clearly did not want to be seen with Ellis, an understandable precaution to take. They had only met once in person, at the same cabin. All the rest of their conversations had been electronic, as had been the transfer of money to Ellis for services rendered.

Ellis was confident because of his ironclad position. He had Lowry in his pocket, and Lowry was the one indispensable part of the operation. Without Lowry they had nothing.

But Ellis would have been in a great bargaining position even without Lowry because Ellis knew what was going on, and the conspiracy could only succeed if kept totally secret. One word from Ellis to the authorities or the public would blow it all up. Ellis's knowledge was by itself worth a small fortune. Or maybe not so small.

But Ellis was careful, a trait that had kept him alive and healthy in the violent world in which he lived. He had seen and dealt with pretty much everything anyone could throw at him.

Lowry, Ellis knew, was untested in matters like this, so he wanted to prepare him for any eventuality. That's why he arrived at Lowry's house to pick him up an hour earlier than necessary. They would plan exactly what they would say and how they would act in the crucial meeting to follow.

Lowry seemed nervous when Ellis arrived, which was completely understandable. Lowry had waited a long time for this, much of it spent in a cell with nothing to do but think. It would all come down to today.

The two men agreed that Ellis would do the talking. He would explain the changed situation calmly and completely, stating the conditions and the financial terms. The employer would be upset and would probably ask for time to consider this new information.

Ellis knew that would be just a delaying tactic, a way to play for time. But time would not help them, not with the cards that Ellis and Lowry had to play.

Ellis barely gave a thought to the possibility of a physically violent reaction. Not only could they not dream of being able to handle him, or the ex-boxer Lowry, but it would do them no good anyway. What would they do? Kill Lowry? That would mean the end of their operation.

"Are we clear on everything?" Ellis asked, when it was time to head out.

"I think so," Lowry said. "Yes."

"You feeling good about where we are? Still want to do it this way?"

Lowry nodded. "Absolutely. I deserve my share."

"Good. Let's go."

The drive to the cabin took almost an hour. It was secluded in the woods; the long dirt driveway was more than a tenth of a mile. Ellis had been here before, so knew where he was going.

They arrived ten minutes before the scheduled time, and the lack of any cars outside indicated that they were the first to arrive. When they got out of the car, Ellis looked warily around. There was no chance of ambush, not with Lowry so necessary to them, but it couldn't hurt to be careful.

Seeing no sign of anyone, Ellis looked into the cabin through the window, again out of an abundance of caution. The place was empty and had been for a while; dust was gathering on the wooden table that could be seen from the window.

"Let's go." Ellis opened the door and went inside.

The bullet hit Ellis directly in the center of his forehead; he was dead well before he hit the floor. Even though Lowry should not have been surprised, he was, and he recoiled in horror. With the exception of the man he had hit in the bar, he had never before seen anyone die.

"Holy shit," he said to himself, since he hadn't even seen the killer yet. That changed moments later, when Radoslav Duric appeared in the doorway off the bedroom.

"Here are your instructions," Duric said, opting not to start with "Hello." He handed Lowry a piece of paper, which simply said, "You did well. Go home and wait to be contacted." So Lowry left, happy to leave the cabin and especially Duric behind.

Lowry drove down the driveway. Marcus, in hiding, had to decide to either keep following him or wait to see what had happened to the person Lowry had come with. Marcus also wanted to see whom they had met.

So when Duric came down the driveway, Marcus snapped his picture. Marcus then walked to the cabin, through the woods so he could not be seen, to find out what had happened to Lowry's friend.

"GET OVER HERE RIGHT AWAY," LAURIE SAID WHEN I PICKED UP THE PHONE.

"What is it?"

"Corey, please come here now."

I hung up the phone, put Simon in the car, and raced over there. She's on the porch to greet us, and I see Andy in the doorway behind, waiting as well. Neither of them looks happy.

"I'll start at the beginning," Laurie says. "Marcus just called; for the last couple of days he had been following John Lowry. I wasn't aware of it, but Marcus has good instincts."

I nod. "Good. I should have thought to do that."

"Me too," she says. "So he just called; he followed Lowry and another man to a cabin about an hour west of here. He was able to photograph the man."

She holds up her phone and shows me the photograph; it's not someone I recognize.

She continues, "Lowry left a few minutes later, alone. Marcus decided not to follow him; he was more interested in finding out who else was in the cabin. His reasoning was that he knew where Lowry lived, and he could always resume surveillance later on.

"Another car followed Lowry out less than a minute later, driven by a different man, not the one Lowry arrived with. Marcus was able to get a photo of him as well."

She shows me this photo, which is slightly blurred and a bit hard to make out, since it was taken through a windshield of a moving car. But I can tell that it is also not someone I am familiar with.

"Marcus waited there for about an hour, apparently at the end of the only road or long driveway leading to the cabin. When there was no other activity, he made his way through the woods, unobserved, to get a closer look. There was no sign of anyone being in there, so he approached the cabin carefully and looked inside.

"The original man that Lowry arrived with was on the floor, his head basically blown off by what must have been a bullet in his head. He didn't go inside; there was no one to help and I'm sure he didn't want to take a chance on leaving prints or DNA."

"Did he notify the police?"

"Yes. He called nine-one-one anonymously after he left the area. There's nothing in the media about it yet, but I imagine there will be soon."

"So let's think about what we have here. Lowry is expanding his criminal portfolio; he obviously led the first guy into a murder. The fact that he was allowed to just drive away demonstrates that. The second guy was the executioner."

"We need to find out who these people are," she says. "The media will be telling us the identity of the victim."

"And we need to go to the authorities," I say. "We have

evidence in a murder case. This is not just about defending our client anymore."

"Agreed. Andy, what do you think?"

"The murder was apparently committed in an unincorporated area," Andy says, "so it's a matter for the state police. I would go to them. Laurie and I have a good contact there."

"What about the SEC or FBI to report what we know about the overall operation?" I ask. "Whatever they're doing is clearly about to happen."

Andy shakes his head. "I would say no. They will either put it on the back burner or take forever to investigate it. And they would be heavy-handed; whatever is going on, the conspirators could go underground and wait for a more opportune time. I think you're better off staying on it yourselves; you can always report it whenever the situation changes."

"Aren't we withholding evidence of a crime?" Laurie asks.

Andy shakes his head again. "You don't have evidence of a crime. You have suspicions, but you don't even know what the crime is. I don't see any obligation to report."

"You want to set up the meeting with your contact in the state police?"

"I'll do it," Laurie says. "He's not real fond of Andy."

Andy nods. "I am tragically misunderstood. I can only hope that history will judge me fairly."

"I wouldn't count on it," Laurie says.

NEW JERSEY STATE POLICE CAPTAIN ROBERT DESSENS LOOKS PISSED OFF.

I've got a feeling that is not exactly breaking news; he seems like the kind of cop who always looks pissed off. I know the type; I was that type. I probably still am.

He also does not seem to be a big fan of Andy Carpenter's. That does not make him unique among New Jersey cops. Except for perhaps serial killers and pedophiles, defense attorneys head every cop's list of reviled professions. Andy obviously is not the exception to the rule . . . not even close.

But that Dessens is seeing us on such short notice reflects that he respects Andy as a serious guy. They've had dealings before, and Dessens apparently knows that if Andy and Laurie say something is important, it's not going to be a waste of Dessens's time.

The murder victim was found in the cabin, and media reports identified him as Ellis McCray. Few details are given, other than that he was originally from Detroit. I expect that Dessens already knows much more than that; whether he will share any of it is another matter entirely. But that's okay; we're here to give information, not to receive it.

"Okay, to what do I owe this honor?" Dessens asks. "And what could be so important it requires three of you to say it?"

"Laurie and Corey are here to protect me from potential police brutality," Andy says.

"Don't think I'm not tempted. What have you got?"

"You found a murder victim in a cabin north of here. The media identified him as Ellis McCray."

"Tell me something I don't know."

"That will be easy." Andy hands Dessens a printout of the photograph Marcus took of the man who followed Lowry in leaving the cabin. "He's the killer."

"Who is he?"

"No idea." What Andy doesn't say is that Laurie has sent the photograph to an FBI friend of hers in Boston, asking if she can help in the identification. "Hopefully you can run it through your super-duper face identifier."

"It's pretty blurry," Dessens said.

"He was leaving the scene of a murder, so he apparently didn't want to stop and pose."

"Who took the photograph?"

"Our partner Marcus Clark."

"What was he doing there?"

"Working on a case," Andy says.

"And the details of said case?"

"That's privileged and separate and apart from the murder. But he was on the scene, or more accurately near the scene, and he took the photograph. Maybe you can do some investigating on your own."

"We're going to want to talk to Marcus Clark."

Andy laughs. "Good luck with that. I've been trying to do that for years. But he will make himself available."

Dessens nods. "Okay. You got anything else?"

"Just a question. Who is Ellis McCray?"

Dessens starts to say something, then stops. My sense is he was going to tell us it is none of our business, but caught himself. "Sure, why not? He was a hired gun out of Detroit. Actually, that's not giving him enough credit; he was a hired anything. Multitalented, very high priced, dangerous guy."

Dessens holds up the photograph we gave him. "If this guy took him down, then you can assume he's more talented, higher priced, and extremely dangerous."

We head back to Andy and Laurie's house, and a message is waiting from Laurie's contact in the FBI, Cindy Spodek. She wants Laurie to call her back "ASAP," which is as promising a group of letters as we could hope for.

Laurie calls her back and asks if it's okay that I pick up the extension and take part in the call. Spodek is fine with it, so I do so.

Spodek gets right to the point. "His name is Radoslav Duric and he's a Croatian national. Let me put it another way: we think his name is Radoslav Duric and we think he's a Croatian national. He operates under so many fake names and uses so many fake passports that it's impossible to know for sure what is real and what is fake.

"He is available anywhere in the world to the highest bidder, and he is dangerous in the extreme. There are seven different Interpol notices out for him from seven different countries. We are not one of those, but we want him very badly. To our knowledge he has never operated in this country, but can I assume you are in the process of adding to our knowledge?"

"You can definitely assume that. He committed a murder that the New Jersey State Police are investigating. We just provided them with this photo, so they don't yet know who it is they are dealing with."

"They'll find out soon enough. Tell me more."

Laurie and I tell Spodek basically what Andy told Captain Dessens. We leave out the specifics of what we are investigating because we don't want the FBI blundering in and alerting Sloane that he's under intense scrutiny.

"Our agents down there will be all over this," Spodek says. "They may want to talk to you guys."

"Always happy to cooperate," Laurie says.

"They will want to know more about your investigation."

"Not everybody gets what they want," Laurie says.

JOHN LOWRY HADN'T LEFT HIS HOUSE SINCE THE INCIDENT AT THE CABIN. It had left him stunned and angry at himself for being so foolish and naïve. He had told his bosses about Ellis's visit to the jail, and about his pitch to Lowry that they demand far more money. He had not trusted Ellis and was not about to possibly throw away all he had worked for in a greedy and heavy-handed scheme like that. He saw in Ellis a danger to the plan, rather than a way to make it far more profitable.

But as amazing as it seemed to him now, he did not realize he was luring Ellis to his death by bringing him to the scheduled meeting. He did not know what was going to happen, but murder never entered his mind. He was dealing with financial people, not the types to get their hands dirty, and not the types to countenance cold-blooded murder.

Or so he thought.

But it didn't get more cold-blooded than what he had

witnessed in the cabin. He did not know who the killer was, or what his connection was to the conspiracy. But to Lowry, who had spent seventeen months in a prison filled with violent criminals, Ellis's killer was the scariest person Lowry had ever seen.

The whole encounter had left him in a panic and unsure what path to take. The conspiracy required his presence to monitor the program and to renew it when necessary. Lowry's fear was that they might force him to reveal the techniques; the guy in the cabin obviously was capable of a violence that could force Lowry to do or say anything. But once he gave them what they wanted, they would kill him. He had no doubt about that.

Or he could take his large cash advance and go on the run. But they would still need him, so they would find him. They had the resources to do or find anything or anyone. He was sure of that as well.

Going to the cops seemed out of the question. He would surely go back to jail. He couldn't handle that again. Not that he would be there for long, since his ex-partners turned tormentors would get to him. There would be no limit to their anger or their desire for revenge.

For now he could only do what they wanted, pretending that their partnership was as firm as always, and that he trusted them. They were ready to proceed and had instructed him to put the plan in motion.

So there he was, at his computer, having entered the password and seeing his handiwork open in front of him. It was foolproof, the work of a genius. He was proud of it, even took the time to admire it, but he could take no pleasure in it.

One way or another, it was going to cause his death.

So he did what he had no choice but to do.

He pressed the button.

WAITING IS SO HARD BECAUSE WE DON'T KNOW IF WE'RE WAITING FOR anything.

It's been almost a week since we met with Captain Dessens and told the FBI about Duric, and no one has contacted us. Dessens had a detective interview Marcus, which I'm sure will go down in state police annals as the least productive interview ever.

But nobody has contacted us, which is incredibly frustrating. For all we know the financial operation, whatever it is, is in full bloom. We have no way of knowing, and no obvious way of stopping it.

This just doesn't work for me. I'm used to being out on the street, pushing and pulling, making things happen, sometimes making mistakes.

Passivity is not my thing. Pressure is my thing.

We've been focused on what we don't know, but we do know plenty. Whatever is going on, we know who is running it, who is participating in it, who is making it happen, and where it is happening. In order, those answers are Miles Sloane, the eight investors who sent him $1.5 million each, John Lowry, and Equi-net.

That knowledge could scare them into making a mistake, but I'd feel better if we had a better understanding of the possibilities and the players. Laurie agrees, but I'm clearly the one to handle it, since I have had the most involvement with this group already.

My first stop is to again visit with Drew Lockman, ex-partner of Miles Sloane's. Lockman knows the terrain and hates Sloane for making him take the fall and nearly go to jail for an investment fiasco. His acquittal in Judge Henderson's courtroom did not in any way remove his resentment of Sloane.

We're meeting again in his River Edge apartment. He's dressed the same as he was the first time I saw him, jeans and a pullover sport shirt. I guess when you don't work and you live in a fancy apartment, it doesn't matter what you wear.

"So, are you making progress on whatever the hell you're trying to make progress on?" he asks.

"More than you'd imagine, not as much as I'd like."

He nods. "Believe me, I know the feeling. So you want to talk about Miles Sloane?"

"How did you know?"

"Well, last time we talked about Sloane and Arthur McKnight and Kevin Vickers, and as far as I know, Arthur is still a rich son of a bitch and Vickers is still dead. I doubt much has changed with them."

"Good analysis. By the way, I talked to Vickers's girlfriend, Denise Tennison; thanks for setting that up."

"No problem. Was she helpful?"

"She told me that Vickers was working for Sloane when he

was killed, which was a piece to the puzzle. I'm still missing a bunch of other pieces."

"I'm here to help. I sure as shit have nothing else to do."

"Thanks. Let me tell you what I know. Sloane is involved in some kind of scam to make a great deal of money. It involves some kind of computer manipulation and the Equi-net company." There is no reason to share the rest, such as that the "gang of eight" have sent $1.5 million each into Sloane Enterprises. Lockman is still technically a silent partner in that company, and I don't want to give him any reason to make noise . . . at least not yet.

He is frowning as I'm talking. "Doesn't make sense. Don't misunderstand, Miles Sloane is a piece of garbage who would kill his grandmother to make a buck. But he's not a computer guy, and—"

"There's a computer guy on board."

"—and the Equi-net piece doesn't make sense."

"Why not?"

"Here's the short version. You have ten shares of IBM and you want to sell them. You have a price you want to get. I want to buy ten shares of IBM, and I'm willing to pay the price you want. I give you a check for that amount, and you give me the shares. Simple, right?"

"Right."

"That's all that Equi-net does. Their computers match buyers and sellers, the deals are done, and everyone goes away happy. How do you scam that? If somehow the computers are giving Miles Sloane a better deal, which is not possible, then someone else is getting a worse deal. You don't think they'd complain? If you said you would only sell a stock if you got ten bucks, you think you'd be okay if they sent you a check for nine?"

"I understand all that, and on the surface it's perfectly logical. But there's something there."

"Did you talk to Equi-net?"

I nod. "I did, and the very nice lady there told me I'm full of shit. Her systems people checked into it and found nothing."

"There's nothing to find would be my guess as well. You could go to the SEC, but they'd probably laugh you out of the building. At the most they'd check with Equi-net, who would just tell them what they told you."

"You know Sloane; how would he react if I confronted him?"

Lockman thinks for a few moments. "Obviously depends if you're right or not. If you're wrong, he denies everything and thinks you're an asshole. If you're right, he denies everything and clams up. I don't know what the scam is, but he'd likely put it on hold until you give up trying to figure it out. Either way, you get nothing out of it, except maybe the pleasure of seeing him squirm."

"Then I'll definitely do it, because making him squirm at this point will be very pleasurable."

Lockman shrugs. "Big mistake, but you're the investigator. I'm the involuntarily retired financial guy."

He's probably right that confronting Sloane would be a mistake, and I might decide not to do it. But right now that's not what I want to hear. It's a trait of mine that when I hear things that I don't want to hear, I deliberately stop hearing them. In this case that's easy to do, so I just thank Lockman and leave.

MY GUESS IS THAT ELLIS MCCRAY KILLED KEVIN VICKERS.

It seems logical that Ellis was the hired gun employed by the conspirators. Then Ellis likely tried to overstep, possibly along with Lowry, so they hired Duric to get rid of Ellis.

They probably can't get rid of Lowry because they need his talents. If they get to the point where they don't need Lowry, his remaining life expectancy would be about twenty minutes.

I ask Laurie if she's heard anything from Pete Stanton about progress in the Vickers murder case. She and I both doubt that there will be any because Ellis was a pro and unlikely to leave anything incriminating behind. But Laurie is going to call Pete to get an update and to tell him our suspicion that Ellis is the killer. If Pete agrees, then the case will quickly wrap up. There is no sense arresting someone who has already had his head blown off.

In the meantime, I decide to talk to Denise Tennison, Vickers's girlfriend, for a second time. I should have asked her the first time if she knew whether Vickers kept any kind of calendar or daily diary that she might have access to. I don't even know whether they lived together, but she has said they were dating for three years and planning marriage.

I don't have her contact information, so I call Sam Willis and ask if he could get me her phone number. Since Sam could probably use his computer to get the national nuclear weapon codes, getting a phone number should be within his skill set. All I have is her name and that she works at Applebee's, and he promises to get right back to me.

He calls back in a half hour, which knowing Sam is twenty-eight minutes longer than I would have thought it would take. "No such person."

"Excuse me?"

"There is no one by that name in this area, and no record of her at Applebee's."

"Which Applebee's did you check?"

"Why do you insult me? I looked at the pay records of every Applebee's within a hundred miles, as well as their corporate payroll."

Sam had obviously accessed private records illegally, but I seem to be growing increasingly comfortable with that. I'm on a slippery slope to full-scale criminality; by next week at this time I'll probably be shoplifting cans of tuna.

I start to ask whether Sam is sure, and whether he tried various potential spellings of her name, or whether she uses a married name . . . those kind of things . . . but I know enough about him to know that he's done it all.

I thank him and hang up. I have no idea what to make of this. The person who claimed to be Denise Tennison might have been operating under a fake name, and she might have lied about where she works. Possibly she did all that so I could not track her down, but this person willingly met with me the first time. I don't think I said anything to scare her off, and she gave me her name and employer before we even met and talked.

I don't know what to do next. In my experience, investigations create their own paths to follow. One thing leads obviously to the next; each step is dictated by the one before it.

This case is different. It is a series of dead ends and roads that double back on themselves and lead into dense shrubbery that feels impossible to cut through. I feel like I'm in constant need of a machete.

Fortunately, this time my next step is planned for me. Cynthia Warren of Equi-net calls with a simple message:

"I need to show you something ASAP."

"AS I TOLD YOU, OUR SYSTEMS PEOPLE HAVE FOUND NO ISSUES ON OUR end," Cynthia Warren says once I'm settled in her office. "Everything seems to be fine and in working order."

"I have to say that is not quite the breaking news I was hoping to hear."

She smiles, but without humor. Then, "But I've been keeping track of trades initiated by the eight companies that you mentioned to me, and I have found some concerning data."

"That's more like it. Tell me about it."

"I probably shouldn't. This is not technically secret information; all trades are by their very nature public. But our customers have some expectation of privacy, so I would ask that you exercise as much discretion as possible. The fact is that you anticipated something like this, so I am seeking your input as much as providing information."

"I understand." I would pretty much say anything to move this along.

"The eight companies have had a rather unusual trading pattern this past week. I don't mean necessarily unusual in the big picture relating to the entire market, I mean unusual compared to their previous actions. What they have done this week is markedly different from anything they have done before."

"In what ways?"

"Well, for one thing, their trading volume is up. Not wildly so, but enough to be noticeable. For another, they are doing quite well. As a group they were up two percent, while the S&P was down almost a percent. That is a very significant difference. Every one of the eight companies made a profit this week, which is statistically off the charts in this market."

"Anything else?"

"Yes. The majority of their trades have been very short-term; in almost all cases they have bought and sold within hours. That is how day traders act, and these companies have never been day traders before. I can show you everything I've just told you."

She hands me a series of charts that do just that—they prove that everything she has said is true. Even my untrained eye can understand a chart where the performance of the eight companies is a graph line going up, and the overall market is a graph line going down.

"What is the percentage likelihood this is by chance, without any manipulation going on?"

She thinks for a moment. "If I picked eight companies at random and found this, I would say one percent. The fact that you had mentioned these eight and anticipated some issues reduces that down to much closer toward zero."

"Have your systems people reexamined your network in light of this news?"

She nods. "They have. According to them, there is just nothing there. I'm going to have to alert my bosses in the main office. This is more than I want to be responsible for."

"Wait a couple of days. Please."

"Why?"

"I think by then I will have more information for you to convey to them. If I don't, then you can still plunge full speed ahead."

"Two days. Then I send this material in."

I nod. "Fair enough."

I leave and call Laurie.

"This really pisses me off," she says. "We're sitting here watching as they're doing exactly what they want, killing anyone who gets in their way, and raking in money."

"My sentiments exactly."

"Time to go on offense."

"What have you got in mind?"

"We make things very uncomfortable for Mr. Lowry."

MARCUS HAS BEEN WATCHING LOWRY ON AND OFF.

The goal was to catch him meeting with Sloane or another coconspirator that we don't yet know about. That hasn't happened; according to Marcus, Lowry has been holed up at his house, going out only for groceries.

We had planned to go after Lowry earlier, but the Ellis killing delayed that. Now it's time, and Laurie and I head for his house. I bring Simon along because we want to scare and intimidate him. Simon is good at that.

We knock on the front door and Lowry opens it. He's a big guy, an ex-boxer, so likely a tough guy as well, but he looks scared. I don't mean of us necessarily, even though we are not what one would expect to show up at one's house. He looks scared on a different level, and I'd bet it's been going on for a while.

"Mr. Lowry, we want to talk to you."

"What about?"

"We'll tell you when we're inside." I step into the house with Simon, and Laurie follows; Lowry makes no effort to stop us.

Once we're in, Lowry says, "You can't just force your way in like that."

"All evidence to the contrary," I say. "Here we are."

"Who are you?"

"Concerned citizens," Laurie says.

He looks warily at Simon, who is not exactly happily wagging his tail. "Is that dog dangerous?"

"Frequently."

"John, we have a situation here," Laurie says. "You are in a bit of trouble."

"I haven't done anything wrong."

"No one said you did," she says. "That's what we call a tell. You revealed yourself, but it doesn't matter, because we already know what you did. That is why we're here."

"I don't know what you're talking about."

Laurie shakes her head, as if saddened by his pitiful denials. "Perhaps we can help you with that. You've illegally interfered with the Equi-net computer system so that a group of wealthy yet very unsavory individuals can prosper. In the process, a number of people have been murdered. You, in fact, either witnessed or committed the murder of Ellis McCray, who you brought to the cabin where it took place."

"Is this jogging your memory any, John?" I ask.

He is clearly past petrified and heading toward frozen with fear. "I have nothing to say."

Laurie shakes her head. "Wrong answer, John. When we leave here, we are going to the FBI. They will dismantle the whole thing and send everybody away for a very long time, including you. You think seventeen months felt long, John? Wait until you experience it for the rest of your life."

"John, the smart play is for you to go with us, for two reasons. Number one, if you give up what you know, what you did, and who you did it for, you will absolutely be able to cut a great deal for yourself. You get a good lawyer like Walter Cummings again and you could even walk.

"Number two, do you know who you are dealing with? Your bosses kill everyone who has information that can hurt them. You are the mother lode of information; do you think they are going to let you ride off into the sunset?"

Watching his face as he listens to Laurie, I think he's going to crack. He doesn't, but he comes close. "I need time to think."

I jump in here. "John, I've got to tell you, thinking doesn't seem to be your specialty. If you were any good at it, you wouldn't be in this situation. This time you should listen to your gut; it has to be telling you that there's no other way out of this."

"Okay," Laurie says. "We'll cut you some slack. We'll give you until eight o'clock tomorrow morning, and then we bring in the FBI."

I hand him my card. "Call this number anytime before eight A.M. tomorrow. After that, don't bother, just sit tight. They'll be coming for you."

When we leave, Laurie asks, "Do you think he'll call?"

"I think he should, but I doubt he will. I wish he was smarter."

JOHN LOWRY WAS FORMING A PLAN.

He was starting to come up with it while those two people and the scary dog were in his house, but after they left, he carefully weighed his options and came up with his strategy.

He simply could not go to his employers and tell them what had happened. They were volatile and extremely dangerous, and they would view Lowry as compromised. They would likely decide to kill him, after first forcing him to give up the knowledge that only he had.

Or they might not do that, but instead facilitate his going into hiding. But he could not trust them to decide whether he would live or die.

He could also not go to the FBI with these people. First of all, they were not in a position to guarantee him any kind of a deal. But even if they were right, and the system went easy on him for cooperating, he could still get a long time in prison. Ten years? Twenty?

He simply did not know, but he could not risk spending the bulk of his life in prison. It was just a different type of death, a life not worth living.

So the other option, the only option, was to run and hide. While he had previously considered it almost impossible to successfully pull that off, he was changing his mind.

He figured he had the two things that were essential to hiding in the modern world. He had money; if handled prudently, the advance that he was given for the operation could last for a long time. Lowry had no desire to live expensively; he just wanted to live.

The other thing he had was a brain and incredible savvy in technology and computers. That he was even in this position was proof of that. But the way you hide in the technological age was to lose yourself in cyberspace. He could create a totally new identity for himself, a totally new life.

He had to give it a shot.

So he set to work, carefully packing the things that he would need, mostly clothing and his computer devices. By 10:00 P.M. he was ready to leave, and he started loading the car, which was in his garage. He finished doing that before discovering that someone else was in the garage, waiting for him.

Radoslav Duric.

At 10:05 Duric took Lowry back into the house.

At 10:18 a crying Lowry agreed to write out all he knew about the Equi-net project, including passwords and detailed instructions.

At 10:41 he finished writing it.

He died at 10:43.

LAURIE PICKS ME UP AT SEVEN THIRTY IN THE MORNING FOR THE DRIVE TO Lowry's house.

He did not call last night, which didn't come as much of a surprise. We're checking a box this morning by giving him one more chance to change his mind, but we both think it's a waste of time.

This time I don't bring Simon with me since whatever intimidation we might have accomplished we took care of yesterday. Obviously it didn't work as planned.

As soon as we pull up, it's clear that something is wrong. The garage door is open, as is the trunk of the car inside. That's where Laurie and I make our first stop. We see three suitcases and a computer case packed in there.

"This is not going to end well," Laurie says.

We go to the house and ring the bell. When there's no answer, we do it twice more. The door is locked, so we go around to the back and try the door nearest to the garage. It's open.

"Let's go in," she says.

I agree, thereby adding trespassing to my list of crimes. If we were still cops, I'd think we had probable cause to enter without a warrant, since I think we are going to discover a body. We're not cops and we are warrantless, but legalities like that are not going to stop us.

There is no sign of Lowry or anyone else, nor is there any indication of foul play. We walk through the entire house, looking for any clues as to what happened to him. His bed is made and not slept in, and there is nothing to make us think that he ate any breakfast.

The closets and drawers are less than a third full, and I have a feeling that the missing items are in the car. "He was bailing out," Laurie says, realizing I'm sure that she's stating the obvious.

"Until someone interrupted him."

Laurie nods. "One way or the other they decided that they don't need him anymore. It seems not to be a good idea to be on the list of people that they stop needing."

A pen is on the floor next to Lowry's desk. I point to it. "It's possible he wrote out what they needed to know."

"Under duress. Severe duress."

"We might have been the reason they killed him. They could have had him under surveillance, and when they saw that we showed up, they might have been afraid he would talk to us."

She nods. "He wasn't going to. He was going to try and disappear."

"Well, he's accomplished that. He is never going to be found, unless they want him found."

"We should make a missing person's report."

I shake my head. "We can, but the cops won't take it seriously yet. You know as well as I do, an adult missing for a few hours is not exactly Amber Alert material. And there's no evidence here of violence, although the cops wouldn't enter this house anyway. They would need a warrant, unlike us."

"They're getting rid of all the people that can hurt them," Laurie says. "Once they do that, they can sit back and run their scam forever."

Laurie is right. Based on the numbers that Cynthia Warren showed me, the eight companies are making a nice profit, but nowhere near the money necessary to justify what has gone on. I imagine part of the reason is that they don't want to call attention to themselves by overdoing it, though since I don't know what they're doing, that's just a semi-educated guess.

But what she has just said gives me an idea. "You're right; they are getting rid of everyone who could hurt them. And now they can just sit back, unless they get drawn out by going after someone else who can hurt them really bad."

"I sense a terrible idea coming on," she says.

"It's not terrible, and you know it. Let them come after me, and we'll be ready for them."

"What will that accomplish? They'll send a hired gun, be it this guy Duric or someone else."

I nod. "Probably. But if we can get our hands on that person, maybe we can work our way up the ladder."

"We know where the ladder leads. It leads to Miles Sloane."

I smile. "Exactly. And that's where I'm going."

THE PHONE RINGS AT SIX O'CLOCK IN THE MORNING.

It's on Dani's side of the bed, and she picks it up and looks at the caller ID. "It's Laurie."

"Uh-oh." This is either an amazingly realistic déjà vu moment, or another big problem.

I take the phone. "Who died this time?"

"Miles Sloane."

"I was kidding."

"I'm not. Pete called me and gave me the details; he said the media will be running with it any minute. Sloane was found last night; he had been missing for almost twenty-four hours."

"Cause of death?"

"That's a little complicated. His car went off the road and down into a gully. It was hard to see from the road because of the dense shrubbery; Pete said it was lucky that it was found when it was. He doesn't appear to have died from the accident; at first look the coroner thinks it was a heart attack."

"Did he have a heart condition?"

"Apparently so."

"Does anybody on this call believe that Miles Sloane died of natural causes?" I ask.

"Not unless there's a third person listening in."

"So my confronting Sloane wouldn't seem to be an effective plan anymore, if it ever was. We need to come up with something else."

"If Dani doesn't mind, we can discuss it at dinner tonight. Oh, by the way, happy birthday."

Those two sentences prompt a whole series of possible questions from me, such as "We're having dinner tonight?" and "Dani is going to be there?" and "It's my birthday?"

Instead I go with "What the hell are you talking about?"

"Uh-oh," Laurie says. "I didn't realize it was a surprise."

"What surprise?" I notice that Dani is cringing while overhearing this.

"Talk to Dani, and tell her I'm sorry for blowing the surprise."

I get off the phone and reflect on its being the first time in my entire life that I forgot my own birthday.

"Don't be pissed," Dani says. "I thought you'd like a night out with friends, so I set it up. It's just a simple dinner at Dantoni's with Laurie and Andy."

I didn't even know that Dani knew Laurie and Andy. My instinct is to complain about this; I hate when people pay attention to my birthday. I especially hate when people do things behind my back, even when they are well-intentioned. But I don't want to be an asshole; Dani went out of her way to do something nice.

It's going to happen anyway, so there's nothing to be gained by acting like my normal, idiotic self.

It's possible I may be maturing.

So I go along with it. It's an early dinner, six thirty. I find that the older I get the earlier I like to eat. If this keeps up, I'm going to have to move lunch and breakfast earlier as well, so as to maintain space between meals.

I spend the day unproductively thinking about what to do next in our case, and also following the media reports of the death of Miles Sloane. The coroner has confirmed that he had a heart attack while driving. I suppose it's possible; maybe the stress of what he had been doing got the better of him. But I doubt it.

Sam Willis calls to give a report on Denise Tennison's whereabouts. I had asked him to do whatever he could to track her down. I can tell that it pains him to say it, but he's still come up empty: "She does not exist on this planet."

We get to the restaurant, arriving at the same time as Andy and Laurie. They hadn't met Dani before; she had just called Laurie because Dani knew that we were friends. They seem to hit it off instantly, and I'm sure Laurie will be disappointed when Dani and I stop seeing each other. I will be also.

I will? I didn't realize that until I just said it to myself. Maybe I should think this through.

So we have a thoroughly pleasant dinner. Laurie and I have agreed we shouldn't talk about work, so instead we talk about everything else. It's an easy, comfortable, fun conversation of the type I have not had in a long time.

We order dessert and it comes along with a cupcake with one candle on it. This sends everyone including the waiters into an awful, embarrassing rendition of "Happy Birthday to You." Mercifully I don't have to sing along.

A few minutes later I ask Andy if he saw any of the Mets game. It started at 4:00 P.M. because they were playing the Dodgers on the West Coast.

He just about jumps out of his seat. "Don't tell me anything!"

It's a bizarre reaction. "Don't tell you anything about what?"

"The Mets game."

Laurie chimes in with an explanation. "Andy taped the game because he couldn't watch it live. And he placed a bet on it, so he wants the exquisite agony of watching his money go down the drain, pitch by pitch."

"You're going to watch a game that's already over?" Dani asks.

Andy nods. "I am."

"So everybody else will already know whether you won or lost, including the person you bet with?"

"It's called a bookmaker, you sheltered person, you."

"Do you win a lot of money?"

Laurie laughs, and Andy says, "What's so funny?"

"Andy would find a way to lose even if he was able to place the bet after the game was over."

I haven't contributed to this banter because my mind has spent the last thirty seconds alternating between racing and being stunned. But it's my turn now. "That's it."

"That's what?" Laurie asks.

"I know what's happening."

"Are we talking about the case?"

I nod. "We are. Listen to this . . . ."

THE ATTENDEES AT THE FUNERAL SERVICE FOR MILES SLOANE ARE A WHO'S who of the financial industry.

At least that's what it seems like to me. Since I have no idea who is who in the financial industry, I can't be sure. But there must be three hundred people here, and every man is wearing a suit that I'm sure costs more than my entire wardrobe.

I'm glad but not surprised to see Drew Lockman here. He hated Sloane and blamed his ex-partner for his going on trial and almost to prison. But he's shown up to say good-bye.

People tend to honor their enemies in this way when the enemies die. Even though the people are secretly glad that the enemy is dead, they know that they will look good for being there. It feels like a big gesture, even though it's anything but.

First of all, when the person you hate dies before you, you've won. Victory is assured, you have outlived the bastard. So you go to the service more to gloat rather than to honor, yet you also get the credit for somehow being a big person who is looking past your anger in the face of this tragedy.

It's a win-win.

Also here is Arthur McKnight, who was actually close to Sloane and who invested at least a small portion of his billions with Sloane's company. I would assume that every one of Sloane's competitors is angling to get a piece of that money before Sloane is even in the ground.

McKnight and Lockman don't even acknowledge each other, at least not as far as I can tell. They hate each other; Lockman thinks McKnight tried to put him in prison, and McKnight thinks Lockman stole his money. Whichever of these two guys dies first, you can be sure the other will be at the funeral service.

The service is going to begin in about twenty minutes, so Laurie and I just hang out talking to each other. Everybody else seems to be working the room, probably working out secret financial arrangements that will enrich each other at the expense of peasants like myself.

When the peasant revolution begins, these are the kind of people I am going to be coming after.

Lockman does not exactly seem to be the center of attention. His legal troubles have left him something of an outcast, and certainly a line of people are not waiting to chat with him.

I walk over to him. "Come to say good-bye to your buddy?"

He smiles. "Why not? We had a lot of good years together."

"Are you going to give the eulogy?"

Another smile. "No, I don't think so. We also had some bad years."

"You and I should talk."

"Again? I've talked to you more than my ex-wife."

"That was different. Those times I was looking for information. Now I'm looking for something else."

"What's that?"

"A piece of your Equi-net scam."

He's pretty good; I've got to give him that. He doesn't react with any kind of shock or surprise, nor have I succeeded in wiping the smile off his face. "I don't think I know what you are talking about."

I nod. "Maybe I wasn't clear enough. I am talking about the Equi-net scam you have been running. If we have time, we can also talk about the murders you have been directing to keep the scam going. But the good news for you is that I don't want to bust it up; my goal is to keep it going. Then maybe I can afford the kind of suit that everybody here is wearing."

The lights in the room flash on and off, indicating that it's time for us to go in, that the service is beginning. "Here's all the information," I say, handing him a piece of paper. "We are going to meet and negotiate our terms in a place where your friend Duric can't show up with a weapon to take me out. Although if he did that, you'd probably show up at my funeral and pretend we were buddies."

Lockman looks at the paper, then at me. "You have no idea what you are talking about. You know nothing."

"Really? I don't think I ever told you this, Lockman, but I'm a movie buff. Buffs know a lot about their subjects. Did you ever see a movie called *The Sting*? If not, watch it and then decide if I know what I'm talking about. But show up for our meeting, or the next time the jury won't go so easy on you.

"Now smile so my partner thinks we're buddies. She doesn't know what is going on; she wouldn't like what I'm doing. She's hung up on morality."

With that I turn and walk back to Laurie. Without either of us saying a word, we walk into the service.

IN THE OLD DAYS, YOU COULD GET TO AN AIRPORT GATE WITHOUT A TICKET. Not only that, but you didn't have to take off your shoes or run your possessions through an X-ray machine or stand in a futuristic booth and hold your hands above your head while they take a photograph that removes your clothing so a bunch of uniformed agents in some room somewhere can ogle or mock your body.

But one advantage to the new airport world we live in is that one can be fairly confident that the traveler sitting in the seat next to them is not carrying a handgun. It's comforting when meeting with a murderer, which is what I am hoping to do.

My note to Lockman told him to buy a ticket to any United flight out of Newark and meet me at Gate 17. I picked the number in honor of one of my favorite movies, *Stalag 17*. It took place in a prison camp, though I doubt that Lockman will make the connection or appreciate the irony.

I spent yesterday afternoon talking to Sam Willis about the computer scam, then to Andy's broker about some stock market trading processes. They were helpful to me in fleshing out my understanding about what I believe has gone on. I can't be sure that I'm right; I certainly don't yet have direct evidence.

But I'm at Gate 17 right now, and if Lockman shows up, it will be all the confirmation I need.

And here he is. He is smiling and appears confident, though he must know that he is in deep shit. Everything he has worked for could go down the drain if this meeting does not go the way he wants it to.

"I'm here because I'm curious as to what the hell you are talking about," he says, standing over me.

"I'm happy to enlighten you. But you want something first? Maybe a Cinnabon?" I point to the Cinnabon bag on the little table next to me. "I shouldn't have these; they are way too fattening for me; when I eat one of these, it looks like someone stuck an air pump in my ass."

He sits down next to me at the only available seat, on the other side of the little table with the Cinnabon bag on it. He disregards my gracious offer of the Cinnabon. "Say what you have to say."

"Did you watch *The Sting*?"

"No."

"I'm going to assume you're lying. But it doesn't matter. The movie is about con men running a sting, where they rip off a rich bad guy for half a million dollars. Isn't that quaint? Back in those days half a million was a lot of money. It was Newman and Redford, four years after *Butch Cassidy*. Those guys were good; not many movie stars like that around anymore."

Lockman doesn't say anything, obviously hoping I'll stop babbling and get to the point. Which I am about to do.

"You and your conspirators have been doing what is called past posting. In horse racing, as shown in *The Sting*, it means betting on a race that has already been run, when you know the winner. It's pretty tough to lose that way. John Lowry set up a system to do it in stock trading."

Getting no noticeable reaction from Lockman, at least outwardly, I continue, "No need for me to get too detailed on this; you know it better than I do. But with computer trading being what it is, we are talking about milliseconds. Basically, you're buying stocks that have already gone up."

"How did you figure it out?"

"I'm really smart. But Lowry was even smarter; killing him might have been a mistake. But too late now."

"What do you want?"

"I told you at Sloane's funeral. By the way, how did you kill him and make it look like a heart attack?"

Lockman ignores the question. "What do you want?"

"I want a piece of what you're doing. I'm not greedy; a hundred grand up front, and fifty grand a month for the rest of my natural life. The upfront money in cash; after that I'll have set up some kind of account in an island somewhere, maybe like you did with Judge Henderson in the Caymans."

"Is that all?"

"I should have asked for more?"

"I meant, is that all you have to say?"

"Pretty much."

"How do I know you won't take this and hit me up for more?"

"You murdering blackmailers aren't very trusting. I, on the other hand, am a man of great honor." I hand him my card. "Call me when you want to arrange payment, or when you want to turn me down. I can successfully deal with either outcome."

He takes the card, puts it in his pocket, and walks away. I wait five minutes, pick up the Cinnabon bag with the microphone in it, and leave as well.

PETE LISTENS TO THE TAPE, THEN REWINDS IT AND LISTENS AGAIN.

Laurie, Andy, and I have heard it a bunch of times, but I know that I personally never get tired of it. "We've got him" is what Pete finally says.

"It's not enough, but it's a damn good start," Andy says. "If you just confirm some of the financial details, that should do it. He has a separate fund set up within Sloane Enterprises. It was walled off so that Sloane couldn't access it; that was part of the deal when they split up. So when the money came in from the other conspirators, Sloane wasn't even aware of it."

"Are you sure they killed Lowry?" Pete asks.

Laurie nods. "That's the way they operate. You can and should put out an alert and search for him, but my guess is he's already buried. When they want you to find a body, they sit it in front of the high school. When they don't, then the body disappears."

"By the way, what are you doing here?" Pete says. "The Feds and the state police would be dying to make this collar."

"We feel really close to you, old buddy," Andy says. Then, "It was Laurie and Corey's idea; I told them you'd screw it up."

Pete nods. "I'm not surprised."

"There's a lot more we can tell you," I say. "You should have the full background before you go in."

"I'm all ears."

Laurie and I lay out what we know about the conspiracy, including the eight other privately held investment companies that are in on it.

"But I still don't understand how they are making the money," Pete says. "How do they buy stocks at the lower price after they've already gone up?"

"If you're asking how Lowry's computer program works, I have no idea. Even Equi-net's systems people couldn't find it. But I can tell you what it does. You want to sell a stock. You can either just sell it at the market price, which means whatever it's currently trading at is fine with you. Or you can put in a limit order. For example, you say you want ten bucks a share, and if they can't get you that, you're not selling."

Pete is just listening and nodding.

I continue, "Now keep in mind that these computer trades happen in milliseconds. You hit Send on the trade, and by the time you check your orders, the trade might well have been done and you have your ten bucks.

"So let's say that stock moves up, in that moment, from ten dollars to ten dollars and twenty cents. Lowry's computer sees that and quickly buys the stock at the ten dollars you asked for. Keep in mind again, it's a fraction of a second, so you have no idea the stock ticked up; you're getting the price it was at when you made the trade.

"You're happy with your ten bucks, and the buyers have already made twenty cents, which is two percent. Now if they want, they can sell it back right away; making two percent in less than a minute is pretty damn good. Or, they can hold it for a while with a two percent head start.

"If you investing many millions over many years, that two percent becomes an absolute fortune. And that was the idea; this was going to be an annuity that would last forever; there was no chance it would be detected. Lowry was brilliant."

"I'm going to have to bring the Feds in anyway," Pete says. "They have the financial experts to deal with this; we're just a bunch of dumb cops."

"I've been saying that for years," Andy says.

"Bring them in on your terms, Pete," Laurie says. "They back you up, but you call the shots."

He nods. "You can count on that."

"But we want to be there when you move in," I say.

"You can count on that too."

THIS IS THE MOST I'VE MISSED BEING A COP SINCE I LEFT THE FORCE.

Laurie, Marcus, and I are at Lockman's apartment building as Pete and his team prepare to take him down. They have confirmed with the doorman that he's at home, and they're about to move in. I wish we could be active participants, but I realize that we can't.

I've brought Simon with me for old times' sake, but he is going to be as uninvolved as we are. We're forced to wait downstairs while the current cops do their job.

So they move in. I don't know exactly how they're going to do it, and I'm not going to get to see it. It's a shame; I'd love to see Lockman's face when they show up. I hope I'll get to see him in handcuffs as they take him out.

A half hour goes by. I'm not surprised it's taking this long; Pete will be careful so as to limit the danger to his team. Laurie's cell phone finally rings and she answers. "Now? Is it over?" She listens for a few moments. "Damn."

She hangs up. "Pete says we can go upstairs."

"Did they get Lockman?"

"No, but someone else did. He's dead; strangled with his neck broken. His body is in the shower."

"Duric," I say, as we go up the elevator. I bring Simon with me because I am not about to leave him alone downstairs. Marcus doesn't come up with us; he nods his good-bye and melts away.

There's nothing to see in the apartment. Pete's diagnosis of Lockman as dead is accurate. As the place fills up with people from forensics and the coroner's office, we head for the door.

Pete stops us just before we make our exit. "Be careful. They know that you know their secret."

I nod; I had already thought about this. One of the motives for confronting Lockman directly was to get them to come at me. If they do now, I'll be ready. Simon and I will both be ready.

When we get downstairs, Laurie says, "If this was Duric, and it probably was, then there is still somebody paying his salary. Lockman was not in charge, or at least he had a partner, and that person was willing to sacrifice Lockman for the cause."

"You're right; Lockman may not have been top dog. It could be one of the investors. But the Feds will get to the bottom of it. We've done our part."

"Pete is right. You could be next. It makes sense."

"I understand. Don't worry about me."

Simon and I head home. The house is dark, as I left it. I had turned on the alarm system, so I'm feeling pretty confident that no surprise is waiting for us as we enter.

We go inside and Simon immediately sits up straight, alert and signaling to me some danger. I was obviously wrong about everything being okay, because if I've learned one thing, it's to take Simon's warnings at face value. I take out my weapon and do a pointing gesture to Simon, which means "Stay."

I start to inch my way into the hallway. It could be nothing, but I'm not going to take any chances. I hear a slight noise and think it's Simon, so I turn to where I think he is.

The bullet hits me just below the shoulder, the impact sending me back against the wall and to the floor. I look over and see Duric. He must have disabled the alarm and was waiting for me.

He starts walking toward me, pointing his gun. He is going to get closer so the next bullet can go into my skull. The look on his face is not angry or eager or human. It is cold and empty.

There is simply nothing I can do; I had dropped my own gun when the bullet hit me. Duric stops walking and raises his weapon.

I am about to die.

Simon soars silently through the air and lands on Duric, just the way he used to when he was working the street. Duric screams in pain as Simon latches on to his arm, digging his teeth into Duric's flesh. I try to get up to find my gun, but the pain in my shoulder is excruciating. I fight my way through it.

Before I can get to it, I see that Duric has picked up his own gun in his left hand as Simon chews on his right arm. Duric points the gun toward Simon. He is going to shoot him and I can do nothing about it. I feel a wave of fear and nausea unlike anything else I have ever felt.

Suddenly there is a gunshot, and in the confusion I realize that Duric is not the shooter. He is no longer holding a gun at all. Across the room is Marcus, holding his own gun. He has literally shot Duric's gun out of his hand. Until this moment I thought the only person that could do that was the Lone Ranger.

"Simon, here," I say, and Simon comes over to me and lowers

his head. He saved my life, and as a reward all he wants is to be petted.

Marcus holds the gun on Duric and walks toward him. Marcus doesn't touch him; all he does is kick Duric's fallen weapon toward me. Marcus then comes over and hands me his own gun. Marcus could just as easily have shot Duric in the head or through the heart instead of in the hand, but he intentionally did not do so.

Marcus wants to do what I did to Renny Valdez, which is get revenge, one on one. And I bet he's doing it for the same reason that I did; first Renny and now Duric tried to kill Simon.

Simon is on our team; we have his back.

Marcus now walks back to Duric, who is one scary guy in his own right. I know what he has already done, and I know from Laurie's FBI friend how dangerous he is.

I hope Marcus can handle him. I'm hoping, but not worrying, because if Duric seems like he is going to come out on top, I'm going to shoot the son of a bitch in the head.

Duric lands the first blow, a kick to the side of Marcus's head. Duric is incredibly agile for a man his size.

He goes to kick Marcus again, but Marcus grabs his ankle and yanks it farther up in the air, sending Duric crashing to the ground. Marcus twists Duric's leg, turning it into a human corkscrew, and Duric gasps in pain.

Marcus lets go and Duric scrambles to his feet. This time Marcus doesn't wait for him to make another move. He throws a straight left jab into the area that used to be Duric's intact nose, then throws another left into his chest. I can hear the thudding noise when these punches land; I have no idea how Duric is still standing.

Soon he isn't. When Duric leans over in reaction to a gut punch, Marcus hits him in the Adam's apple with a right elbow.

Duric goes down like he was shot, gurgling and moaning. Either his larynx is made of cast iron or he is going to spend the rest of his life making squeaking sounds when he talks to his fellow inmates.

The bad news is that I am not going to get to shoot the son of a bitch.

ANDY HAS A TRADITION THAT HE FOLLOWS WHEN HE WINS A CASE.

He throws a victory party at Charlie's Sports Bar for everyone involved in the effort. Even though there was no jury verdict in our investigation, it still feels like a win, so we're at Charlie's tonight, continuing the tradition.

I invited Dani to the party because, I tell myself, she contributed greatly by saving Simon's life in her discovery of the poisoned steak in the backyard. The real reason, I don't tell myself, is that I want her here because I am crazy about her.

So in addition to Laurie, Marcus, Andy, Dani, and me, Pete Stanton and Sam Willis are also here. Andy's friend Vince Sanders is on the scene as well. He's the editor of the local newspaper, and Andy says that Vince is so devoted to free food and beer that if he wasn't invited, he would have crashed the party anyway.

Also at the party are Willie Miller and his wife, Sondra. They are friends of Laurie and Andy's, and Willie is Andy's partner in the dog rescue that they run.

Last but definitely not least, Simon and Tara are also here; the manager of Charlie's has graciously allowed it. Sebastian, Andy and Laurie's basset hound, preferred to stay home and sleep.

The party is to honor the memory of Judge Henry "Hatchet" Henderson, and Pete Stanton has been instrumental in ensuring that his reputation is being restored.

Pete has uncovered frequent contacts between Drew Lockman and Peter Tuckman, the PR guy for the court system, who along with Judge Pletka was in Henderson's inner circle. Lockman had paid off Tuckman for his help; Tuckman had received more than $100,000 for his efforts.

Tuckman has caved and told what he knows and what he did. His efforts were significant and tragic. He gave the blackmailers Henderson's cell phone number and his upcoming trial schedule, even though that information had not been made public.

Vickers was killed because Laurie had told the Judge that we were going to confront Vickers that night, and he had mentioned it to Tuckman. The blackmailers were afraid that Vickers would reveal that he was working for Lockman, so they made sure that couldn't happen.

Most significant, Tuckman had secretly left the back door to Henderson's house unlocked when he, Pletka, and Henderson met on the fateful night that Henderson died. So there was no forced entry. There isn't any proof, but the Judge was extremely likely murdered, most probably by Ellis. We are going to make sure the public knows the truth.

I am happy that everyone now believes that Henderson did nothing wrong. When he wouldn't cave to the blackmail, the blackmailers went to plan B, which was to kill him and let the case fall to Judge Pletka.

They were confident that Pletka would let Lowry out. That was partially because Tuckman conveyed to them Pletka's view of the case, but more important because they knew that the system would bend over backward to be fair in cases that Henderson had handled. With judicial error being alleged in the Lowry case, and Maria Burks missing as a witness, Lowry's release was virtually assured. Andy had predicted exactly that.

The conspirators waited eighteen months to get Lowry out because they needed time to set up their investors. Lowry behind bars was the safe approach, so that he could not do anything else stupid to jeopardize the operation.

Laurie and I haven't had time to reflect on the way the case went down; I've spent a day in the hospital having my wounded shoulder treated. Simon has stayed at Laurie's house with his friend Tara.

"How did you know it was Lockman?" she asks.

"I wasn't sure, but the pieces all fit. He had a separate fund within the company, which Sloane didn't see. He also still had a phone line and number in the company system which allowed calls to be forwarded to him, so while we thought that Vickers had called Sloane, he was actually calling Lockman.

"The worst part is that I was probably responsible for Sloane being murdered. I had mentioned to Lockman that I was going to confront Sloane with the information of a scam involving the Equi-net systems. He tried to talk me out of it, and when he couldn't, he ordered Sloane killed. If Sloane had lived and taken my claims seriously, he might have uncovered everything.

"Also, Lockman set me up to talk to Denise Tennison, who pretended to be Vickers's girlfriend. She was a fake, and he must have known that. They were setting Sloane up to take the fall if anything went wrong, which it did."

"I just wish we knew who had Lockman killed. I hate to see someone like that walk," Laurie says.

"If it was one of the investors, the Feds will take them down for the financial crimes. Evidence of murder might be tougher to come by; Duric is not the type to talk. But I'm afraid we need to let it go and let them handle it."

Laurie nods. "I guess so." Then, "You did good."

"The team did good. Especially Marcus, who took it upon himself to watch out for me. He saved my life and Simon's life. I thanked him a little while ago, and he said, 'Ynnhh.' I couldn't have put it any better."

Dani walks by us and Laurie says to me, "Dani is terrific."

I shrug. "I guess."

"Don't screw this one up, Corey."

"We'll see what happens."

"Corey, let me ask you a question. How would you feel if she dumped you?"

I think about it for a few moments. "Like shit."

Laurie smiles. "Exactly."

I'M AT ANDY AND LAURIE'S HOUSE TO COLLECT MY PAY.

We had gotten a retainer from Judge Henderson, but when he died, Andy assumed financial responsibility for our work. I argued the point, but he said that he wanted to clear Henderson's name if at all possible, and if he didn't hire us, he'd hire someone else.

"I'm not happy about this," I say when he hands me the check. "You shouldn't be paying us."

"Get over it. You guys did an amazing job. I could have done better myself, but not that much better."

"Humble as always." I look at the check; it's more than I earned in two months as a cop. "I would invest this if I knew I'd make a profit. Maybe we should have kept Lowry's program running."

Andy shakes his head. "Wouldn't help much. You'd need a lot more than that to get started. The scheme only worked because the investors had huge money going in. A two percent profit, even in only a day, only really matters if it's two percent of big bucks."

Laurie overhears us talking and says, "I know about the other conspirators, but where did Lockman get that kind of money?"

"Maybe he used the money that each of them put up," Andy says. "It was like an initiation fee into the club."

I shake my head. "Sam had kept his eye on the company records. He said that money wasn't touched."

Laurie and I both think of it at the same time, but she says it first. "Let's call Sam."

IT HAS TAKEN THREE ENDLESS DAYS TO PUT IT TOGETHER.

That is not in any way Sam's fault; he accomplished everything we asked of him in less than six hours. The delay came when we asked the legal authorities to perform the same work, without revealing what Sam had done. They move a hell of a lot slower than Sam, partially because they need to get warrants and other annoying inconveniences.

I am sorry to say that I have been won over; I am a Sam Willis groupie.

So we've come to Manhattan ready to put what we've learned to productive use. Last time I came here alone and I was stuck in the reception area for a half hour, reading magazines. This time Laurie and I are ushered right in; that's the advantage of bringing two cops and two FBI agents with us. We don't have to wait for the receptionist to say, "Mr. McKnight will see you now."

The cops and agents let us go in first, without Arthur McKnight even knowing they are here. I'm wearing a wire, but it doesn't matter. Nothing he says will be necessary to prosecute.

He seems surprised to see us, but unruffled. "To what do I owe this visit?"

"Arthur, this is Laurie Collins. Laurie, Arthur McKnight. I thought you should meet Laurie because she's really the one who figured out that you are a lying, murdering piece of shit."

Rather than looking scared, his face and eyes take on a cold and angry look. "No one speaks to me like that. Now I don't know what you want, but you had better leave now."

"No problem," I say. "All we wanted was to tell you that you are about to be the wealthiest inmate in the history of the federal prison system. You will be able to buy all the cigarettes that you could ever want."

"You have nothing."

It's Laurie's turn. "Here's what we have. We have financial records between you and the eight conspirators; each of them was using your money for half of their investments, with you getting half the profits. The cops flipped the CFO of Sloane Enterprises, who made sure that Lockman's fund was completely shut off from Sloane, so that he couldn't see what was going on. He has implicated you and provided records. You had only pretended to resent Lockman's losing your money; it was just a head fake to insulate you from him. And we're just beginning. Corey, did I miss anything? Do we have anything else?" She turns to me.

"Just one thing. We also have a reception area full of FBI agents and cops that are here to arrest you. My only regret is that Judge Henry Henderson won't be the one to send you away for the rest of your life."

The agents and cops come in and make the arrest. I'm sure

McKnight will hire the best lawyer that money can buy, maybe even Walter Cummings.

But it won't help.

Chalk one up for the K Team.

Read on for a sneak peek at the next book in the K Team series

ANIMAL INSTINCT

LISA YATES WAS TRYING TO LIVE NORMALLY.

That's what she was telling herself, although the truth was that she was merely trying to appear as if nothing was wrong. That was not easy to do, because something was very wrong, and there was no longer anything normal about her life.

Lisa Yates was terrified.

She had been living with that fear for a long time. She finally decided that she would face it directly, but doing so was an extraordinarily risky proposition. This was not necessarily an act of courage, because she believed, knew in her soul, that not doing anything was even more dangerous.

The other thing she knew was that success depended on no one suspecting what she was planning. She was afraid to do it alone; something like going to the police or FBI scared her. She had decided she needed a lawyer, but did not know who to approach. And she had to be extraordinarily careful in whatever she did.

They could well be watching.

So this was intended to seem to be a normal evening out. She had no desire to go out; her inclination was to stay at home, obsess about her situation, and go over her plan for the thousandth time. Instead she'd spend a couple of hours making small talk, more for show than to help her forget her dilemma. Nothing could get her to forget.

So she went out to dinner with Una Loge, a former colleague at work who had left when she got married. Lisa had stayed fairly close with Una and her husband, Dave, but Lisa's own domestic situation by its very nature kept them somewhat apart. Lisa's domestic situation, at least until a month ago, was a train wreck.

They went to Manero's, in Teaneck. While pretending to be attentive and in the moment, Lisa let Una do most of the talking. But while Lisa was physically present, her mind was a million miles away.

The dinner took a little over two hours. Lisa revealed nothing about herself, not even sharing stories about the office, though Una still knew most of the people there. Una could tell that something was wrong and inquired about it, but when Lisa said that everything was fine, Una backed off. She wanted to give her friend space but was clearly worried for her.

Lisa quickly grabbed the check when it arrived, more in desperation to end the dinner than to show generosity. She had to get out of there, her mind was exploding, and she couldn't pretend anymore. She told Una that she could pay next time, though Lisa doubted there would be a next time.

They said good night at the restaurant's front door and Lisa walked to her car on the street, not more than fifty feet away, while Una stayed behind, having used valet parking.

Lisa had just reached her car when she heard the noise. In that split second, she knew what was happening, but she did not have time to react, and she did not feel the bullet pierce her skull.

She would never be afraid again.

I am staring fear in the face; it is coming at me in waves.

I don't mean that as a metaphor; the waves are literally coming at me . . . one after another, in varying sizes and strengths.

I am standing at the water's edge of the Eighth Avenue Dog Beach in Asbury Park, New Jersey. I rarely came to Asbury Park as a kid; in those days it was in decline and disrepair. I never understood how that could happen to a city with such a large and beautiful beach; it would seem to be a prime real estate location and immune to such a fate.

But the municipal decay was an unfortunate fact, so for our vacations, the Douglas family always went a bit farther south, to Long Beach Island. Since then Asbury has made a remarkable comeback and is now a thriving community . . . and the dog beach is cool.

So here I am.

With me at the moment are Dani Kendall, who I can no longer deny is my serious girlfriend, and Simon Garfunkel, my longtime pal and partner. Simon is a German shepherd and functioned as my K-9 comrade on the Paterson police force for almost eight years, before our recent simultaneous retirement.

My earliest fear in life was as a result of my first trip to the beach. I was with my mother and brother, and we were staying in a boardinghouse on Long Beach Island. We used to go there for a two-week vacation every summer, but my father would come down only on weekends. He was a sergeant in the Paterson PD, and he worked overtime as much as he could. I can never remember him taking a weekday off. Even taking Saturday and Sunday during our vacation was a major concession on his part.

I was probably four years old and excited to be going in the ocean for the first time. Then my mother killed that feeling of anticipation by warning me of the undertow, or riptide, or whatever she called it. It was an invisible, mysterious force in the water capable of dragging small children off to certain, horrible death. And, according to her, it was relentless and overpowering; once a child was in its grip, it was over.

So the four-year-old Corey Douglas did not go in the ocean that day, or any day since. Literally never; I've always considered the downside to be too great.

It's not a phobia. The dictionary defines phobia as an inexplicable or irrational fear. That doesn't apply here; it's very rational to be afraid of being dragged to one's death by the ocean monster known as riptide.

The irony is that I have spent my life attacking and overcoming fear; as a cop the criticism most often levied at me was that I was not cautious enough. I think that's fair; I took it as a badge of honor that I didn't let being afraid stop me from doing something. In fact, it provided an extra impetus.

I've also discovered that when you refuse to give into fear over so many years, then you stop having to make the gesture of refusing, because you stop being fearful. The trick is to remain careful and cautious without that fear as a motivation.

But I've never gone into the ocean, and I'm never going to. That has remained a riptide too far.

"You going in?" Dani asks.

"Not in this lifetime." She knows my feeling about this, but was just checking to see if I'd bite the bullet.

"What about Simon?"

"He and I have discussed it, and he shares my views on the matter."

She holds up a tennis ball, one of a half dozen that we've brought along. "Should I try?"

I nod. "Fine with me. But you're wasting your time. Simon and I are land animals."

Dani rears back and throws the ball into the water, getting it maybe thirty yards in. As she does, she yells, "Go get it, Simon."

And he does.

He plunges in like he's been doing it all his life; all he's missing is a surfboard. I have no idea how he does it, but within thirty seconds he's got the tennis ball in his mouth and is heading back to us. He drops the ball at Dani's feet, triumphant.

He looks so damn happy, and I'm glad of that. But my dominant feelings are relief that he has conquered the dreaded riptide, and guilt for having deprived him of this joy his whole life. Simon has suffered because of my reaction to something my mother said to me when I was four.

The sins of the father shall be visited upon the son.

"You learn something every day," Dani says, handing me the ball.

I throw it in, not as far as Dani did because I'm being protective of Simon. Maybe the riptide was backing off the first time, trying to make him overconfident.

He dives back in, repeating the retrieval, and this time dropping the ball at my feet. He looks at me with a combination of eagerness for me to continue the game, and disdain at my personal wimpiness.

At least that's my impression.

"Come on, let's take a walk along the water," Dani says.

"Okay."

"You going to take off your sneakers?"

It hadn't entered my mind, and I notice for the first time that Dani is barefoot. Simon is bare pawed, per usual.

"Do I have to?" I may not be the most free-spirited soul you could run into.

"Of course not; there are no sneaker police on the beach. But most people do. It feels good."

"We're walking in dirt. That feels good? I believe shoes and sneakers were originally invented to prevent people from having to walk in dirt."

"It's sand, Corey."

"That is a distinction without a difference." I think about it for a few moments, then, "Okay, what the hell."

So we have a nice barefoot walk, throwing the ball into the water along the way. I can't remember the last time I saw Simon so happy and exhausted.

"I wish I didn't have to leave," Dani says.

Dani works as an event planner, and she's doing a big corporate gathering in Miami. She'll be gone for a week. "So do I," I say. "But we'll have this dirt walk as a memory to hold on to."

When we're finished, we stop for brunch at an outdoor café. We both like to read the newspaper in situations like this; it's one of the many things I like about Dani. She's comfortable talking or not talking; it doesn't seem to matter to her either way.

We buy a *Newark Star-Ledger*; I take the sports section and she has the rest. We'll trade off as we go along. We order food; she and I each have pancakes and we get Simon a bagel and some scrambled eggs, along with a dish of water.

After a few minutes, she says, "Oh." It is not a happy *oh*.

"What's the matter?"

"A woman was murdered in Teaneck last night."

I'm a cop, or at least I was a cop. Now I'm an investigator, and I'm still interested in these things. "Let me see."

She hands me the paper and I look at the story. The entire newspaper seems to explode in my face; I read for a few moments and then lean back in my chair, trying to catch my breath.

"What's the matter?" Dani asks. "Did you know her?"

"I might have killed her."